BL

TAURUS
 *(April 20 to May 21)*

The material person. Loves the finer things of life. Uses sight, sound, smell, touch and taste to soak up information about everything around her. Patient and practical, once Taurus makes up her mind, she digs in and sticks stubbornly to her course of action.

A Halloween party gets out of control. Loud music, eerie figures of witches and ghouls and a beautiful black satin witch's outfit. Then a fire and an acrid smell of smoke, screams and death. Tess knows how the fire started, she knows who the murderer is. But will her memory return to unmask the killer... and save herself?

*Whatever your sun sign, you'll want to read
Zodiac, the series written in the stars.*

SERIES CREATED BY JAHNNA N. MALCOLM

TAURUS

BLACK OUT

JAHNNA N. MALCOLM

Lions

An Imprint of HarperCollinsPublishers

First published in Lions in 1995

Lions is an imprint of CollinsChildren'sBooks,
a Division of HarperCollins*Publishers* Ltd,
77-85 Fulham Palace Road, Hammersmith, London W6 8JB

1 3 5 7 9 8 6 4 2

ISBN: 0 00 675049 4

Printed and bound in Great Britain by
HarperCollins Manufacturing Ltd, Glasgow.

Special Thanks to Mel Odom

CHAPTER ONE

TAURUS (April 20 – May 21)
The changeable Moon transiting misty Pisces
is fogging your judgement. You've stumbled
on to a mystery with only the vaguest of
clues. Don't jump to conclusions – you may
be wrong. Bite your tongue and wait for all
the evidence to sift in. There is a real surprise
in store for you.

"Ew! Stop!"

Tess Langley felt something like wet sandpaper rubbing across her cheek. She slapped at it with her right hand. Her fingers touched – fur. Yes, that's what it was. Wet fur.

At first she couldn't open her swollen eyes. But when she did, Tess found herself face to face with a soggy black alley cat.

"Gross! Get away from me!" Tess struggled

to sit up. Her head was pounding. Her neck and body ached. She was cold and wet.

"What the—" Tess blinked several times, forcing herself to concentrate on her surroundings. Her back was leaning against a grey metal can full of – she wrinkled her nose – garbage. She raised one hand and saw that a soggy white napkin was stuck to her palm.

"Yuck," she squealed, shaking her arm vigorously.

The scrawny cat that had been licking her face skittered across the asphalt to a collection of trash cans nearby. It eyed her warily as it continued to pick through the pile of rotting food scraps littering the alley.

"Where am I?"

Tess squinted down the alley. She suspected she was in one of the seedier areas of Brookston, Massachusetts. A seacoast town not far from Salem, Brookston's waterfront was filled with pawn shops, strip joints and adult book stores.

"Oh, god, how did I get here?"

She stared at the black satin gown she was wearing. The dress was cut low in the front and fell all the way to her ankles. Tess was wearing a pair of sheer black stockings and the right leg was full of ladders. No wonder. She had on only one pointed black shoe. As well as being soaked from last night's rain, the sleeve edges and skirt hem were singed.

Tess was numb with cold. Her teeth were chattering so violently that their clicking frightened the cat. It backed away suspiciously, shaking its paws to get rid of the soot and water.

She turned her head from side to side and felt a sharp stabbing pain in her forehead. Gingerly Tess touched the spot just above her eye. There was a gash that smarted when she touched it.

"What's happened to me?"

A chill, much deeper than the one she was feeling, filled her body as Tess realized she'd lost something. Something very valuable. But what was it?

Tess struggled to stand and pressed her back against the brick wall of the building behind the trash can. She scanned the area round her searching for...What? Tess couldn't remember.

She shut her eyes and a cloudy memory filled her brain...

It was early last night – Friday. She was in her attic bedroom, standing in front of the mirror attached to her closet door. She checked how she looked in the black satin witch costume, and liked what she saw. The dress was low cut and hugged her curves. She'd tangled her thick black hair so that it looked like a spider's nest. Extra heavy eyeshadow accentuated her round green eyes. She had painted her full lips a blood red, and used an eyebrow pencil to highlight the tiny mole above her mouth.

Satisfied with her appearance, she called her mother and her younger sister Kelly into her room.

"You look beautiful," her mother said. "Maybe a little too beautiful for a high school senior."

Kelly, wearing a dirty blue sweatshirt and matching leggings, smirked and said, "You'd better look beautiful, after all the money you spent on that outfit."

Tess sighed impatiently. "This party at the Hawthorne Mansion just happens to be the biggest deal of the whole school year!"

"That's what you said about the homecoming dance," Kelly needled. "And you'll say that about the prom."

"Don't be so juvenile," Tess said, as she concentrated on fluffing her hair out on her shoulders. "This is the first costume ball I've ever been to. And it's at the Hawthorne Mansion. That is a major big deal."

Kelly bounced on the bed. "Don't be so cranky."

Tess stuck out her tongue at her sister. She was so glad she didn't have to put up with Kelly's teasing all the time. Their parents had agreed to let Tess turn the dusty, unpainted attic into her own bedroom, ending years of having to share a room with her kid sister.

Tess had sewn her own lavender print curtains to match her Laura Ashley pillow covers and quilt, and filled a shelf next to the bed with her collection of tiny porcelain animals from Beatrix Potter stories. Tess occasionally bumped her head on the low, sloped ceiling, but it was a small price to pay to have a room all to herself.

"If that dress was any lower, you'd fall out," Kelly commented, continuing to bounce and shake the whole attic.

"Kelly, stop jumping on my bed," Tess

snapped. "You're just jealous because no boy would give you a second look."

"Yeah, right." Kelly rolled her liquid brown eyes. "I couldn't care less. All boys are totally gross."

Tess stared at her skinny nine-year-old sister, who was convinced fourth grade was the most important time in a person's life, and chuckled. "Check back with me in a few years, we'll see how you feel about boys then."

"Is everyone else wearing such elaborate costumes?" their mother asked, frowning. "I'd hate you to arrive at the party and be the only one dressed up."

"Will you please quit worrying, Mother?" Tess pleaded. "At school, all anyone has talked about for weeks is what they're wearing to the party. Believe me, I didn't spend a fraction of what some of the others girls did. A few paid hundreds of dollars for their outfits."

"Yeah," Kelly cut in, "like Meg, Arden, and Carly – the witches of Brookston."

"Kelly, that's not nice," their mother insisted, swiping at Kelly with one hand. "They are Tess's friends."

"They're hardly my friends," Tess tried to

explain to their mother.

"And they really *are* witches," Kelly insisted. "I heard they have secret meetings and put hexes on people."

"Kelly, really!" their mother chuckled. "I think Halloween has infected your brain."

Kelly turned to Tess. "Remember when they got mad at you and the next day you sprained your ankle?"

Tess's nostrils flared. "It's true that I don't really care for Arden, Meg, or Carly. But I don't think they have the power to make me sprain my ankle."

"That's not what you told me when it happened," reminded Kelly.

"I told you that to make you go away," Tess confessed. "Mom, it was an accident. Not that I haven't had my share of run-ins with Arden."

Tess's mother looked perplexed. "I thought you and Arden were friends."

"Mother, get with the programme." Tess shook her head impatiently. "We were friends in eighth grade. But that was years ago."

"If you really must know," Kelly interrupted, "Arden has never got over the fact that Ryan picked Tess instead of her." Kelly flopped back on the bed. "It's jealousy, pure and simple."

Their mother shook her head. "This is too much for me to comprehend." She tapped Kelly on the head. "Go downstairs and do something constructive, like clean your room."

"On a Saturday night?" Kelly groaned, pulling herself off the bed. "Get real. I'm watching *Creature Features*. It's an all-night marathon."

After Kelly left the room, Tess turned to her mother. "Do I really look all right?"

"You're beautiful," her mother said, helping her fasten her silver chain with the heart pendant. "Now remember, this may be a very fancy party, but I want you home at the usual time."

"Don't worry, Mom," Tess answered. "I won't be late."

Tess snapped back to the present as a garbage truck pulled into the alley. She turned and ran in the opposite direction, crossing a small side street downtown and ducking under some fire-escape stairs in the next alley. She nearly tripped over the alley cat, who was now dragging the bony remains of a fish off to a corner.

"Sorry, kitty," Tess muttered, "But I don't want anyone to see me."

Once under the stairs, she cowered next to an open screen door. Through the wire mesh she could hear the clanging of pots and pans inside. "This must be the Pewter Platter's kitchen," she murmured.

The restaurant was already open for business. It catered to the early morning crowd – milk and newspaper delivery people, truck and taxi drivers, and the police.

Once she realized exactly where she was – a block off the Brookston town square and five blocks from the Hawthorne Mansion – Tess relaxed a little.

She rubbed her throbbing temple, trying to plan what to do next. Her first impulse was to run into the Pewter Platter and ask to use their phone. After all, her parents would be waking soon, if not already, and be worried that she hadn't made it home. But her appearance – she looked as if she'd been in a fight – made her think twice about being seen by anyone. Especially police officers swilling cups of coffee while they ate their steak and eggs.

"The party..." mumbled Tess. She closed her eyes, wondering if she'd even made it there the night before.

"Come on, Tess!" she told herself. "Think! What happened to you last night?"

Memories began to flicker, like electric lights coming back on after a power cut. The memories, though, were dim and short-lasting.

She remembered ignoring her mother's advice to wear something over her black satin outfit. She wasn't about to let some bulky woollen overcoat ruin her entrance at the party. She remembered waiting impatiently in the living room for Ryan to arrive. He was late, as usual.

When Ryan finally arrived, he honked – not even bothering to come up to the door. *I hope it's not going to be one of those nights*, thought Tess. She said goodbye to her family and rushed out of the house.

But when she reached the car, she couldn't believe her eyes. Ryan was sitting behind the wheel of the car wearing a Red Sox baseball cap turned backwards over his short brown hair, a checked flannel shirt unbuttoned over a faded Nirvana concert T-shirt, faded jeans with massive holes at the knees, and grimy basketball hightops.

"What is this?" Tess asked, putting her hands on her hips. "A joke?"

Ryan blinked his dark brown eyes at her. "I could say the same thing."

Tess looked down at the costume she'd worked so hard to make and back at Ryan. "Don't you like my costume?"

He shrugged. "I like it. And so will every boy at the party."

A tiny smile curled her lips. "Oh, do I detect a note of jealousy?"

He leant back in his seat. "No, you're detecting an entire symphony. Now get in, the party starts at eight, doesn't it?"

Tess moved round the side of the car with mixed emotions swirling inside her. Maybe Ryan really was teasing. Maybe he was going to pick her up and then go and get dressed in his costume.

She slipped into the front seat of the car. As he pulled away from the kerb, she said, "I guess you're going to put on your costume when we get to the party, right?"

"This *is* my costume," he joked, flipping on the radio and drumming his fingers on the steering wheel. "I'm going as a high school zombie."

Her face fell. Ryan wasn't kidding. He wasn't dressing up at all. If he wanted to ruin her evening, he was doing a really good job of it. "You don't have to do this," she said in a low voice.

"Do what?" he asked in a totally innocent voice.

Tess wanted to punch him. "Look," she said, trying to stay calm, "why don't you just drop me off at the party and then you can go home and play Nintendo by yourself. That way your evening won't be a total loss."

"You'd like that," he said. His head bobbed up and down in time with the music. "With me gone, you could squeeze up against mister pretty boy, Anthony Stokes."

"What?" Tess frowned at Ryan. "Is that what this is about?"

"I saw you talking to him in the hall today. He practically had you pinned against the wall this morning. And you just smiled and batted your lashes like an idiot."

Tess sighed impatiently. "We were talking about the party. That was all."

"Sure, sure." Ryan gave Tess a sideways glance. "I just want you to know I saw him talking to Rose Flannery in the same way – pressing her against her locker – this afternoon."

Tess shook her head in disgust. "Will you stop getting obsessed about Anthony?" Anthony had only lived in Brookston a few months, but most of the boys at the high school had turned against him. "He can't help it if he's nice looking."

"Nice looking?" Ryan threw his head back and guffawed. "The guy's so thin and washed-out, he looks like an ad for iron-poor blood. But just because he speaks with that stupid foreign accent, every girl in the school drools over him."

Tess tossed her head. "I think Anthony has brought some class to this town. The mere fact that he's throwing this party proves it."

"He's just trying to buy friends," Ryan shot back.

"Well, at least he's trying. The minute he set foot on campus, you and every other jock shut him out. It's really hard having to move in your senior year. But he had to change countries, too. That must really be tough."

"He's got that geeky brother to keep him company," Ryan replied. "He treats him more like a servant than a brother. Always ordering him round."

"Anthony does not order Ian round. Ian likes to help his brother."

Ryan laughed a humourless laugh. "That's what you think. I've seen that look on Ian's face. He resents the hell out of Anthony."

"That's probably because Ian got shorted in the looks category. I mean, it must be hard having a brother who is so suave and handsome—"

Ryan suddenly turned up the radio. "Could we *not* talk about Anthony?" he shouted.

"Who do you want to talk about, Arden Matthews?" Tess shouted back. She couldn't help it. Ryan's petty jealousy was really starting to make her angry. "We could talk about Arden's choice of nail polish – green. Or how about that attractive white stripe she put in her hair? What is she supposed to be, the Bride of Frankenstein?"

"Why does what a person looks like matter so much to you?" he demanded.

Tess tried to make a joke of it. "I can't help it. I'm a Taurus. Beauty is important to us."

"You're a Taurus, all right," he barked. "Absolutely bull-headed!"

"Well, you are an ass!" she shot back. "Look at you. Deliberately trying to wreck the party!"

Ryan slammed on the brakes and the car fishtailed over to the kerb.

Tess had to brace herself to not hit her head on the windshield. "Ryan! Are you out of your mind?"

"You want to go to that party – walk!"

Tess took a deep breath. This was turning out to be one of the worst nights of her life. She waited a few moments before saying quietly, "Ryan, can we talk this over?" She hated it when he lost his volcanic temper but she'd learnt the best way to handle it was to remain calm. "My feelings are hurt because you obviously don't like my costume, which is why I've been so grumpy." She stared down at her hands, clutched tightly in her lap. "I just want you to know this party means a lot to me.

I've really been looking forward to it."

Ryan leaned his forehead against the steering wheel. When he spoke, his voice sounded tired. "Tess? Why did you dress like a witch – when you know it will upset Arden and her friends?"

"Oh, we're back to Arden again," Tess said, slumping down in her seat.

Ryan turned his head to look at her. His voice was low, almost a whisper. "Arden has really changed. Lately she's become very weird – talking about witches and casting spells. It's like she and her friends stepped out of a Stephen King novel. They scare me. The party tonight is the perfect opportunity for them to do something...terrible."

Tess smiled. "What are they going to do? Turn us all into toads?"

Ryan didn't smile back. "You laugh. But I just don't like the whole feel of things."

"Ryan, it's a Halloween party for the entire senior class. Arden and her friends don't have the corner on witches wear. I'll bet a dozen girls will be dressed like me." Tess patted his knee. "Now come on, let's just go and have fun. All of our friends will be there. "

Without looking at her, Ryan put his foot on the accelerator pedal. The car shot ahead towards Hawthorne Mansion.

"You can't say I didn't warn you," Ryan said darkly. "If something bad happens at the party, don't come looking for me."

CHAPTER TWO

*S*omething bad had happened at the party. But shivering in that doorway in the morning chill, Tess could not remember what.

The gash above her eye throbbed. She touched it, expecting to find the wound covered with dried blood. Yet all she felt was the tear in her skin. *No blood?* she thought. *That's weird.*

"We're well ahead of schedule," one of the garbage collectors said. "How 'bout we grab some hot coffee at the Platter?"

"You read my mind," said his partner. "I could use a boost of java myself – especially after last night. I can barely keep my eyes open this morning."

Tess pressed herself into the shadows under the stairs as the men removed their work gloves and tossed them in the cab of the truck.

"Yeah, last night was about the worst I can remember," the first garbage collector continued. "Every volunteer fireman in four counties was called in on that blaze."

The second man nodded. "I got there by eleven – and the thing was already out of control. Talk about an inferno."

Fire? Tess pressed her eyes shut as a glint of memory pierced her mind. *Drapes bursting into flames. Smoke everywhere. Screaming witches and ghouls and skeletons running in all directions, trampling one another.* For an instant, Tess saw herself coughing and choking, desperate for air. Then the memory vanished as quickly as it had appeared.

"Yeah, it was something awful," the first man said. "Seeing the old Hawthorne Mansion go up in smoke like that. And those poor high school kids trapped inside – terrible. You know they found one body – a boy's."

"I heard that," the second man said. "Kid's not even out of high school and – poof! – his life is over. What a shame."

A dead boy? Tess wondered. *Oh my god! Someone died at the party?* She prayed it wasn't someone she knew, like Ryan. Where

25

was he?

Tess wanted to dash out of the shadows and pump the men for details but her instinct told her that wasn't a good idea. She waited until the men entered the restaurant, then, after making sure no one was watching, she bolted out of the alleyway and ran towards the First Church of Brookston. Its simple white spire was visible above the trees across the town square. Tess loved the quiet old church building and right now she needed a place to think.

It wasn't easy running with only one shoe so she stopped to get rid of it. Her stockinged feet found every stone but Tess ignored the pain. Reaching a safe haven was all that mattered. She didn't stop running until she was safely beneath the roof of the church's narrow white porch.

She leant against the railing, trying to catch her breath. Looking down, she saw that the minister's garden – a small patch of ground encircling a simple white cross – had been cleared of dead summer flowers, the earth turned over for its long winter's rest. Seeing it made Tess remember how important the church was to the life of the town.

Before long, it would be time for the church's Thanksgiving service and, a month later, its lovely midnight celebration on Christmas Eve.

Tess spun to look at the church door, confusion knitting her brow. *What was I expecting to find in the church?* It was just another building, and probably not even warm. ("Heat," the minister liked to tease his congregation, "depends on how many living souls occupy the pews.")

The jog itself made Tess feel a little better. Her muscles felt warm from the burst of exertion. And something had drawn her to the church... She couldn't go home now.

Not until she solved the mystery of those eight missing hours in her life. Not until she found whatever it was she had lost.

She loved this church. A simple clapboard structure built in the mid-1700s, it was older than most buildings in North America. It was painted white and its high, pointed steeple was a landmark for miles round. In olden times it had been the spiritual and practical heart of the valley. Marriages were registered and babies were baptized here. Town meetings were still a regular monthly feature. The local dead were buried in the hillside cemetery behind the church.

Tess was about to try the front doors when she heard a noise from round the side of the building. She froze and listened. The sound rattled again. This time she identified it as a jingle of keys.

Tess chanced a quick peek round the corner. It was Reverend Mooney. He liked Tess, but if he saw her now in such disarray he'd probably fall over dead. Determined to avoid him at all costs, Tess hurried round the opposite side of the church.

Hiding there, she felt a strangely warm, low fog wafting from the cemetery grounds. The feel was late spring, not late autumn, and inviting.

The cemetery spread up a hillside dotted with ancient oak and hemlock trees. Some of the gravestones were much older than the church, dating from the late seventeenth century, when Brookston was first settled. Over time, many of these original markers had been eroded and split apart.

Tess could see the familiar Angel of Death carved on more than a few of the remaining graves. The cemetery usually gave her the willies but it was especially creepy this morning since it was shrouded in a low fog.

Tess heard the minister start his car. To reach the road he would have to drive his car right past her. She made a snap decision and hopped over the stone wall of the cemetery. Luckily it was low, and moss provided a soft landing for her on the other side.

Once in the cemetery, Tess decided to see for herself what had happened to the Hawthorne Mansion. She wound her way through the uneven rows to the top of the hill, preparing herself for the worst.

Still, when Tess reached the top, the sight took her breath away.

"Oh no," she whispered.

Below her lay the smouldering ruins of the landmark mansion. Its six brick chimneys stood like lonely pillars. The rest of the once-glorious house was gone, except for the charred skeleton of the roof. A fire crew continued to spray water across the smoking debris, even as investigators were starting a careful search of the area.

Tess had seen plenty of bad fires on television. But nothing like this had ever happened in Brookston, at least in her memory.

Numb with shock, Tess moved along the top of the hill towards the ruined house. She needed to get closer, but not too close. Perhaps if she saw something specific, maybe it would jog her memory about the previous evening.

Desperate, she decided to climb a tree, hoping its higher branches would lend a better vantage point.

Tess had to jump up three times before managing to grab a lower limb and pull herself up into the ancient ash.

She stopped to steady herself. *When was the last time I climbed a tree? I must've been about Kelly's age.* Thinking of her family brought a brief smile to her lips. She knew she had to hurry and get back to them soon.

Tess studied the tangle of branches above her. There was no clear way to proceed. Worse yet, the bark was cutting into her feet. *All you need is to fall out and crack your skull.*

Carefully, she hoisted herself to a higher

joint where two limbs merged, then pulled herself to the next branch. She could see the mansion, but the view was not much better than from the ground.

She climbed to the next level but then she nowhere to go. The higher branches looked too thin to support her weight.

"Great," she muttered, now feeling stuck. "This is just great."

Her chilled legs started to tremble uncontrollably. A freezing wind swirled up suddenly, nearly knocking her out of the tree. The gust carried with it the threat of snow.

"What was that?" she cried, gripping the nearest limb for dear life.

Then a voice called from below.

"Are you stuck? Do you need help?"

Tess looked down and nearly lost her balance. A man stood at the base of the tree, looking up at her. He seemed to have appeared from nowhere.

Tess's first thought was to run. Here she was, alone, with a total stranger in a very cold, very deserted cemetery – and she was stuck in a tree.

Run! The thought was so absurd that Tess

chuckled out loud. She looked down at the man. A boy, actually, about her age. At least he was fully clothed. *And very handsome,* Tess thought. He was wearing dark jeans, black boots and a black leather bomber jacket.

"I didn't mean to frighten you," he called up sincerely. "Are you in trouble?"

"No, I'm fine," Tess called back. "I heard there was a fire at the Hawthorne Mansion."

"Yes." His smile faded. "It lit up the sky for miles."

"I can't believe it," Tess said, feeling the tears about to start. *Great.* Now she was going to start crying. She was already cold, shoeless and stuck in a tree.

"It's been on the television all morning," the boy said. "You can probably see the network TV trucks from where you're sitting."

Tess turned to look back at the mansion and noticed several white vans topped with satellite dishes parked among the fire engines. "Yes, I can see them."

"The firemen think—" He stopped. "Are we going to conduct this entire conversation with you out there on a limb?"

Tess smiled. "It is a little cold up here," she

32

said. Coming down was a lot easier than climbing up. Once she swung to the ground, she was able to study the boy's face.

His dark hair was combed back, unmoving in the breeze. His pale skin only emphasized his penetrating black eyes. He looked a year or so older than her.

"Are you going to a party?" he asked.

"Party?" Tess suddenly realized what she was wearing. She looked from her torn satin dress to the boy and back to her dress again. "Um. Why, yes, I am. A costume party."

"So early in the morning?"

Tess made a snap decision not to tell him about being at the Hawthorne Mansion the night before. Besides, since she had no recollection of the party at all, perhaps she had never arrived. "The party is tonight," she bluffed. "I was just trying out my outfit. What do you think?" She raised her hands in a *voila!* pose. "Do I look like a witch?"

The boy took a few steps back and cocked his head. "Yes, I would say you do." He gestured at the gash on her forehead. "One that's a little worse for wear."

Tess realized how bizarre she must look.

"Oh, that," she said, pressing her hand to her forehead self-consciously. "I, uh, had a spill on my bike this morning. The hem of my skirt got caught in the spokes and pulled me right over."

His eyes looked concerned. "You sure you didn't hurt yourself?"

Tess shook her head. "Just a few bruises. Nothing serious."

Suddenly she felt foolish standing barefoot in rags in a cemetery, talking to a perfect stranger. "Well, I had better be getting home." She started to walk down the hill, but suddenly paused and turned, searching the ground round her.

"Did you lose something?" he asked, watching her spin in a slow circle. "Besides your shoes."

"Yes," she said, a frown creasing her brow. "But I can't remember what."

"A purse," he suggested. "Your keys? Something you wanted to take to the party?"

Tess closed her eyes. *Something extremely important – but what?* She opened her eyes and shrugged. "No. I just don't remember."

The boy thrust his hands in the pockets of his jacket, hunching his shoulders against the cold. "Maybe it's here in the cemetery. I could help you find it."

Tess pursed her lips. She could almost see a picture of whatever it was in her mind. But as quickly as the picture faded in, it disappeared. Tess shook her head to clear the cobwebs. "I can't remember right now. Maybe I should think of something else." She folded her arms across her chest and looked at the boy. "What are you doing out so early?" she asked.

"My favourite uncle was buried a year ago today," the boy replied. "Over there." He pointed to the area of the cemetery where the newer graves lay.

"I'm sorry," Tess murmured.

"He was very old," the boy replied softly. "But I still miss him."

The boy looked so sad and so beautiful that Tess's heart went out to him. "Do you live here in Brookston?" she asked.

"My family just moved here. My uncle left his home to us."

"That's funny," Tess said. "I don't remember seeing you at school." And she knew she would have remembered seeing him, too.

"I haven't registered yet," the boy replied. "I plan to do that Monday."

"Well, maybe we could meet at lunch and I could introduce you to my friends."

The boy nodded. "Thanks." Then he extended his hand. "The name's John Sebastian. But my friends call me by my last name to torture me. I don't mind."

"Nice to meet you, *Sebastian*," she said, clasping his hand. "I'm Tess."

She started to say her last name, but thought better of it. Her world was still out of kilter. *Best to lay low until I can sort things out.* "My father's with the, ah, police department," she fibbed, just to be safe. In truth he ran a music store.

Sebastian flipped up his collar and turned back to look at the Hawthorne Mansion. "I hear the police suspect arson," he reported. "At least that's the rumour going round. Arson and murder."

"Murder?" she repeated. "Someone was murdered at that party?"

"Apparently," he said. "Didn't your father tell you?"

Tess could barely ask the question. "Who

'was the victim?"

"I don't remember the name," Sebastian replied.

"So how do they know it was murder?" she asked, desperate to make sense of this.

"Because they found the murder weapon sticking out of the boy's dead body." Sebastian shuddered. "Gruesome."

"Oh my god!" Tess covered her mouth in shock.

"Awful, I know," the young man sighed. "Absolutely horrible."

"Why would anyone stab him?" Tess asked.

"The party obviously got out of control. That's what the news said on TV." He shrugged. "Who knows? Drugs. Alcohol. Too many people role-playing for Halloween. Something."

"Was there a fight?" Tess asked.

"There must have been."

"Oh, god," Tess moaned.

Something terrible *had* happened, enough for her to blank out the night completely. Could she have witnessed the murder? If so, could the murderer be after *her* now?

"I heard there's still a second kid they can't

account for," Sebastian said, looking back at the burned rubble. "Which is probably why there's still an emergency vehicle at the mansion."

"Another murder?" Tess gasped.

Sebastian shook his head. "I didn't hear. All I know is it's a girl who's still missing."

"A girl?" Tess's heart thudded in her chest. "Do they know her name?"

Sebastian nodded. "Something Langs... dale, um, Langford—"

"Langley?" Tess whispered.

Sebastian snapped his fingers. "That's it. The Langley girl."

CHAPTER THREE

*T*he church door opened just as Tess reached the bottom of the hill. Instinctively she ducked behind a tree. To her surprise she found Sebastian joining her.

"Why are you hiding?" Tess whispered.

"Because the cemetery's hours are posted," he hissed back, "and the minister is very strict about strangers breaking the rules."

Tess tucked her matted black hair behind her ear. "But you're not a stranger. Your uncle was buried here."

"I'm still a stranger. You know how it is in Massachusetts. If you weren't born here and your father wasn't born here, like his father's father, then you're labelled an outsider."

Tess nodded, thinking about Anthony Stokes. He had been actively shunned by most of the boys in her school. She wondered if the same thing would happen to Sebastian.

Tess poked her head out from behind the tree. Reverend Mooney was behaving in a very odd manner. The minister held a tiny vial in his hand. He walked in a circle round the church's back steps, sprinkling water on the ground in patterns.

"It looks like he's making crosses on the ground," Tess whispered over her shoulder to Sebastian. "I wonder why?"

"I've seen that done before," Sebastian said, peering over Tess's shoulder. "I believe it's a ritual performed during autumn."

They watched as Reverend Mooney carefully stepped back inside his circle and folded his hands together. Tess could see the minister's lips murmuring what she guessed was a prayer.

"Isn't that sort of a pagan kind of thing for a minister to do?" she asked.

"That depends on your definition of pagan," Sebastian whispered back. "Many religious rituals, like baptisms – you know, ducking people in water – could be called pagan. Why, Halloween has been called a pagan holiday."

"And that's tonight," Tess concluded.

Sebastian wiggled his eyebrows and lowered his voice. "Allhallows Eve, when spirits walk the earth..."

"Don't! That's creepy."

A sudden gust of wind picked up a pile of orange and red leaves and twirled them in a funnel near their tree.

"Sorry." Sebastian took a step back, surprised at the sharpness in Tess's voice. "I was just kidding," he murmured.

"I didn't mean to snap at you," Tess apologized. "It's just that I've had a strange day."

Sebastian pointed to the clock tower in the town square. The hands read seven o'clock. "But it's only just begun."

As if on cue, the minister finished his prayer and tucked up the collar of his overcoat. Tess watched him check nervously over both shoulders before going back in his church.

"I think it's a strange day for everyone," she murmured.

The church door shut and they heard the faint click of a lock being turned. Sebastian and Tess stepped out of hiding.

"I really need to get home," Tess said.

"Can I walk you?" Sebastian asked.

Tess hesitated, remembering he was a stranger. But then again, if he were intent on harming her, he would have done so in the cemetery, when they were alone and hidden from view. "All right, but hurry," she said, scurrying along the side of the church. "I don't want anyone to see me like this."

Sebastian trotted along beside her, not questioning her when she ducked behind cars or stayed in the cover of the trees. In fact he had barely even mentioned the strangeness of her appearance. Tess looked down at her dress and torn stockings. *What is it with boys? Don't they notice anything? First Ryan doesn't say a word about my outfit and then—*

"Oh my god," Tess gasped, screeching to a halt as they reached the far side of the town square. "Ryan!"

Sebastian stopped beside her. "Did you remember what you were looking for?"

Tess shook her head. "No. It's just that my boyfr—" She stopped and quickly corrected herself. "My friend, Ryan. He was at that party last night. Do you think he could be the one who died?

"No," Sebastian answered. "I overheard a couple of the firefighters talking about it, and I'm certain the dead boy's name was not Ryan."

Tess sighed in relief. She and Ryan definitely had their problems but she would never wish him any harm.

They walked on for a few minutes in silence. He was looking round, perhaps familiarizing himself with the new area.

"How old is Brookston?" he asked.

"It was founded in 1693," she replied. "We celebrated our three hundredth birthday a couple of years ago. But you must have visited if your uncle lived here."

"Well, yes. Maybe once or twice. But my uncle was the real traveller. He usually came to visit my family."

The morning was warming up, but still held the raw chill of a New England autumn. Tess and Sebastian crossed the town park. On the other side, surrounded by woods, lay the Langley family's hundred-year-old house on its own half-acre.

"You mentioned your friend Ryan," Sebastian said, breaking the quiet. "I don't mean to pry but I take it that you're a couple."

"No. Yes. Sort of," Tess stammered. She wasn't quite sure how she felt about Ryan at the moment. All she knew was the previous evening they'd had an argument and the next morning she was lying in a pile of garbage in a back alley. "It's kind of hard to explain," she mumbled.

"Try," Sebastian asked.

"Well, Ryan and I have been together since last summer," Tess said, leading them through the children's playground in the park. A carved pumpkin had been left on the top of the slide and its crooked smile leered down at them as they passed by. "But Ryan has been acting more and more crazy ever since school started this fall. Especially since Anthony Stokes came to our school and—"

Sebastian froze in his tracks. "Did you say Anthony?"

"Yes. Why?"

Sebastian took Tess's arm, as if afraid she might faint at what he was about to tell her. "I think that was the name of the boy who was murdered," he said. "Anthony."

"Anthony!" Tess could feel the blood drain

44

from her face. "Dead?"

"I'm afraid so," Sebastian said quietly.

"That's horrible!" Tess stared unblinking at an empty seat on the swings. The movement was barely perceptible, but it was swinging. Probably pushed by the fierce autumn winds passing through town. Tess watched the swing, her mind racing. "I wonder...I wonder if Ryan had anything to do with—" Tess stopped herself. She didn't want to get Ryan into trouble. Yes, Ryan had a terrible temper and he hated Anthony. But did that mean Ryan was capable of murder? Tess tried to shut the thought from her mind.

Tess started walking once more, forcing herself to put one foot in front of the other. She realized she had never known anyone who died. Oh, the occasional grandmother or grandfather type at their church, but never a close relative or classmate.

Sebastian walked beside her. "Why would anyone want to murder your friend?" he asked softly.

Tess shook her head. "I don't know. He did spend a lot of his time with Arden – an *extremely* weird girl, and her friends Meg and

Carly."

"What makes Arden weird?" Sebastian was starting to sound like a detective probing for information. He noticed Tess look at him oddly, and he shrugged. "I'm just curious. I'm new here. A big fire happens at a party with kids from my new high school. One is murdered..."

His explanation made sense. But Tess wasn't sure that what she was about to say would. "I know you're going to think there's something strange in the water here," she said, "but Arden and her friends believe, or at least they told everyone they believe, in witchcraft. They said they were witches."

"And the other students believe them?"

"Yes." Tess said firmly. She lowered her voice, as if the witches might be listening from behind some tree in the park. "It seemed like bizarre things would happen to people who didn't believe them."

Sebastian chuckled to himself.

"What's so funny?" Tess snapped. "I'm telling you the truth."

"I'm not laughing at you," Sebastian said. "I just can't think of a better place to be a witch. Only a few miles from Salem."

Tess cocked her head, trying to make the connection. Then the light went on. "Oh, you mean, because of the Salem witch trials."

Sebastian touched his nose. "Exactly."

"All of those witches were hung or drowned. You'd think that would frighten them off, but not Arden. She dyed her hair a wild magenta and grew her nails and painted them to look like green talons. Now she roams the halls at school, casting spells on everyone."

"And Anthony liked that?"

Tess shrugged. "I don't know if he did or not. Maybe he thought Arden and her pals were interesting. I *know* they think, er, thought, he was attractive."

They were a few steps from the pedestrian bridge that arched across Brookston Creek, when Sebastian suddenly stopped.

"Is your house far from here?" he asked.

"No," Tess said. "Another few blocks. Why?"

She noticed Sebastian glance at the running water ahead. "Maybe it's best if you go on without me," he said.

"Why? Afraid you'll fall in the creek?" She meant it as a joke. But Sebastian wasn't laughing. Instead, he backed away and was already setting off in the opposite direction.

"I was due home hours ago," he explained.

Tess feebly waved one hand. "I guess I'll see you at school, Monday."

"Oh, you'll see me before then," Sebastian called with a friendly smile. "Maybe out trick-or-treating."

Tess looked down at her ruined costume. "I doubt that."

"Then I'll call you."

"Fine." Tess thought how wonderful it was that she would be the only person he knew when he transferred to her high school. And it would only serve Ryan right if she dumped him in favour of Sebastian.

What am I thinking? I just met this guy and already he's my date for the prom.

A noise sounded at the footbridge. Tess turned to see what it was. A twig had fallen from an elm branch into the creek. Now it made its way like a tiny canoe over rocks and eddies toward the dark shadows under the bridge. As Tess followed the stick's progress, she realized that Sebastian didn't know her last name. How could he ever call her? She spun and called, "I should give you my phone..." Her words died in her throat.

Sebastian was gone.

She looked up and down the path. But there was no sign of him. *How weird. I didn't even hear any footsteps.*

How long had she stared at that stick? The throbbing in her neck and head returned, reminding her it was time – long past time – to go home.

CHAPTER FOUR

*Neptune in Scorpio in the first house makes
you a natural detective. But that same
Neptune also signifies changes and
inconstancy in affairs. With the transiting
Moon, be wary. Look before you leap.*

"Oh, no, the police!" Tess gasped as she
spied the white patrol car parked in front of her
house. She wondered what they were telling
her parents. Obviously they hadn't found her
body in the rubble. *Maybe they've come to tell
my parents that I'm still missing. Or maybe
they think I had something to do with the
murder.*

That thought sent Tess back into the stand
of ash trees at the side of her property. *Maybe
I did and just don't remember it.* She looked
down at her hands that were blotched from the

cold and quivering. *Could I have murdered Anthony Stokes? Never!*

Tess watched the house, willing the police to leave so she could go inside. After a full minute of staring at her front door, she decided she couldn't wait any longer. She needed to go inside, take a hot, hot, shower and talk to her parents, who must be sick with worry.

She moved to the edge of the woods, trying to make as little noise as possible as the ground was covered with heaps of fallen leaves. Tess studied the back of the white clapboard house. It was big and draughty, needed constant repair, but she had loved it.

Tess crouched low, then bolted across the lawn towards the back porch off the kitchen. She raised her head and peered in the window.

No one was in the kitchen – at least no one she could see. Still, it would be too risky to attempt to enter the house by the ground floor. The back door squeaked horribly – her father called it a free burglar alarm – and anyone in the living room would hear it.

She glanced up at the first floor. The curtains of Kelly's bedroom were moving slightly. That meant her window was open.

As quietly as possible, Tess took the extending aluminum ladder down from its hook at the side of the garage. It was crazy thinking she could climb in through the upper floor but what choice did she have?

The ladder weighed a ton, and Tess had to drag it from the garage to the back wall of the house. She anchored it just outside her mother's prized flowerbed, leant the top end against the house, and extended the steps upwards until they reached just below Kelly's window.

The metal was cold on her hands and feet as she hurried up the steps. Reaching Kelly's window, she pushed it up high enough for her to crawl through.

Once inside she planned to hide at the top of the stairs and eavesdrop on her parents and the police.

But her plan went awry the moment she pulled herself through the opened window and fell on top of Kelly, who lay across her bed, weeping.

"Mommy!" Kelly shrieked, covering her head.

Tess clapped her hand over her sister's

mouth and whispered, "Don't shout. It's me, Tess."

Kelly's eyes were wide and bloodshot from crying. She turned her head to look over her shoulder. Tess slowly released her hand and Kelly sobbed, "It's really you. You're alive!"

She flung herself at Tess, hugging her for all she was worth. "We thought you were dead. Mom and Dad, everyone!"

Tess never thought she'd be so happy to see her younger sister. She wrapped her arms round Kelly, squeezing tight. "It's OK, Kell, I'm here."

Kelly released Tess and wiped at her eyes, which were very puffy. She grabbed a tissue from the top of her dresser and cried, "Wait till I tell Mom and Dad, they're going to faint."

Tess dived for Kelly, catching her arm. "Wait!"

"Tess!" Kelly tried to squirm free. "Come on, I want to tell them."

"Kelly, will you be quiet for once!" Tess hissed.

Realizing that her older sister wasn't kidding, Kelly stopped struggling and whispered, "Is there something the matter?"

Tess tiptoed to the bedroom door, opening it just a crack to listen. She could hear voices murmuring in their front room. She slowly closed the door until it clicked shut. "Are Mom and Dad really upset?" she whispered.

"What do you think?" Kelly said. "As soon as they heard the news about the fire, Dad rushed over to the mansion. He was there when they brought out the burned body. Mom and Dad have been taking turns all night going back and forth to the mansion, looking for you. They searched the local accident and emergency wards, even called the town morgue. This is the police's third visit to the house." Kelly stared at her sister. "Tess, you go downstairs right now and tell them you're all right."

"I-I can't." Tess put her hand to the gouge over her eye. "Something's weird. I don't know what it is. But until I do, I need to let the police think I'm still missing."

Kelly pointed to the scratches on Tess's face. "Do you need a doctor?" she asked. "You're all banged up."

"I'm fine," Tess lied. "Somehow, I don't know how, I got out of that burning mansion in the nick of time."

Her sister touched the wound over Tess's eye and behind her ear. "What happened here? It looks like you were stabbed over the eye and jabbed under the ear."

Tess touched her neck, feeling the wound. "Oh, god, I wonder if that cat scratched me."

"Cat?"

"I woke up this morning in a pile of garbage with a mangy alley cat licking my face," Tess explained. "I hope I don't get rabies."

Kelly stared at Tess, tears welling up in her eyes. "We could hear the sirens from here. All of us were in a panic. Then when you didn't come home, we really lost it. I hated thinking how I'd treated you the last time we were together."

"I know," Tess said, her own eyes getting misty. "I'm sorry if I made everyone worry, but it was beyond my control." She tiptoed back to the door and listened. Then she whispered, "Kelly, did you know Anthony was murdered last night?"

Kelly nodded. "I know kids didn't like him, but I can't believe someone would actually kill him. And to end up fried like a breakfast sausage – that's so totally gross!"

"This whole situation is very, very weird," Tess said. "That's why I need to wait until the police have gone."

Kelly narrowed her eyes. "Know what I think? The witches did it – Arden, Meg and Carly. When you didn't come home, I was certain they'd got you too."

"But why would they get me?" asked Tess.

"Oh, come on!" Kelly said. "Arden didn't like you because of Ryan. Meg hates you because you're beautiful, popular and have a boyfriend. And Carly is just plain weird."

Tess blinked in surprise. "You really have been thinking about this."

"You're darn straight. I spent the whole night thinking about that hex Arden put on you just before you sprained your ankle. And that time when you and Ryan were parked, and the horn of his car just started beeping for no reason. You told me yourself Arden did that."

Tess nodded. Practically every one of her friends had experienced a similar strange phenomenon. Lockers that suddenly wouldn't open. Homework that disappeared. Ink pens that exploded all over new outfits. And tripping and falling – over nothing. There had been times when Tess actually believed that Arden might have supernatural powers.

"And Anthony may have been a friend of yours, but let's face it," Kelly continued, "he was the king of those losers. Everywhere he went, Arden and her friends would follow."

Tess's forehead began to throb again. "But if Anthony and those girls were so tight, why on earth would they kill him?"

"Because of something that happened at the party." Kelly threw up her hands. "I don't know, I wasn't there. All I'm telling you is what I heard from Jennifer Rutland, whose sister was at the party. Anthony and Arden had some big falling out."

Tess straightened up, suddenly remembering. "That's right," she murmured. "I remember when Anthony arrived..."

Tess was standing in the marble floored entryway of the Hawthorne Mansion, holding a cup of punch. Loud music blared from the huge ballroom to her right and coloured lights were flashing. Her best friend, Rose Flannery, stood next to her, dressed as Snow White.

"Where's Ryan?" Rose shouted over the loud music.

"At the food table." Tess gestured with her head at the anteroom behind them. "Stuffing his face with his no-brainer friends."

Rose's glitter-covered eyes widened. "It sounds like you two aren't getting along."

Tess took a sip of her punch. "What was your first clue, Sherlock?"

Without warning, the huge carved oak doors at the front of the hallway flew open. In the doorway, back-lit by a streetlamp, stood a tall, elegant figure in a tuxedo and satin cape.

"Wow," Rose gasped, nudging Tess. "Anthony Stokes sure knows how to make an entrance."

Then she caught her breath in alarm. Anthony's face was taut with anger. His eyes flashed as he glared at his younger brother, a cowering, lumpy boy whose Hunchback of Notre Dame costume only emphasized his ugliness.

"Where are they?" Anthony demanded.

Ian Stokes leant away from his brother, one hand raised to protect his head. "I don't know!"

"You fool!" Anthony took one step forward, hissing, "I said, where are they?"

"I don't know. I swear!"

Anthony raised his arm as if to strike, then noticed the stunned expressions on the faces of everyone present. He dropped his arm and burst into a full-throated laugh.

"Welcome," he shouted, throwing his arms open wide. "Welcome, one and all. I hope you enjoyed our little joke."

A burst of relieved laughter ran round the room. Anthony swept into the crowd, greeting his guests with the dazzling charm that Tess had always found very hard to resist.

As if reading her mind, Anthony suddenly appeared before her. His eyes held hers as he bowed and lightly kissed her hand. Tess felt a pleasurable shiver of electricity from the contact.

"Hello, Anthony," she managed to murmur.

"I was hoping you would be here," he purred. "We have so much to say to each other. Perhaps later tonight you and I—"

"Anthony, don't waste your time on her," a girl in a Wild West saloon girl costume declared, slipping between them. It was Marla

Newman, a girl from their school. Taking her role to heart, she threw her arms round Anthony and kissed him hard on the lips. "There, now you're branded. That makes you mine. Let's dance."

Laughing good-naturedly, Anthony let himself be pulled through the crowd towards the ballroom. Just as he slipped through the door he looked back at Tess and, gesturing upstairs with his hand, mouthed the words, "Later."

The phone rang in the Langley house, bringing Tess back to the present.

"Kelly, I *do* remember Anthony's arrival," she gasped. "He seemed to be really angry about something."

"About what?" asked Kelly.

"I'm not sure," Tess reported. "He tried to pass it off as an act but I'm sure it was for real. He said, 'Where are they?' but Ian, who appeared to be really scared of him, said he didn't know."

"They? You mean Arden, Carly and Meg?"

Tess rubbed her forehead. "I can't remember."

"What happened next?" asked Kelly.

"All I know is that Anthony went off to dance with Marla Newman but he seemed to want me to go upstairs to talk...to talk about..." Tess raised her hands, frustrated by her inability to continue. "That's as far as it goes."

"I think this is really important," Kelly said. "Clear your mind. Try to remember."

Tess lay down on the bed and closed her eyes. She tried to fill her brain with memories of the party. Instead, she felt only aches and tiredness in every part of her body.

"Did you go upstairs?" Kelly asked.

Tess concentrated really hard. "Yes. I think so." She shook her head angrily. "Oh! I can't remember!"

"Take your time," Kelly whispered. "Just relax and let your mind drift. OK, it's last night. The party has been going for a while. You went up the stairs – and what did you do?"

Tess was in a room, a candle-lit room, lined with books. The library? Why had she come there? She had been looking for – someone. But she'd been frightened. Badly. And she wanted to run.

Tess started for the heavy oak door but then she heard a sound. Barely perceptible, coming from the far wall. Tess moved cautiously across the semi-darkened floor.

She crossed the room and put her ear against the wood panelling to listen. The noise seemed to be coming from behind a massive bookcase. She pressed closer. Suddenly, the panel she was leaning against shifted – and a passageway revealed itself.

"Tess, don't go any further," a voice whispered inside her. But another voice said, "This is a Halloween Party. Maybe Anthony has turned this into one of those haunted houses. Oh, go ahead, have fun."

Tess stepped into the pitch-black passage, which immediately turned to the right. She could just make out a faint glow in the darkness ahead of her.

She moved towards the light, which grew in intensity. Then Tess heard voices reciting a low, steady chant in a language she didn't recognize.

Suddenly someone or something touched her arm. Tess nearly jumped out of her skin.

"We've been expecting you," a voice

whispered.

The voice was a girl's – soft and inviting. But it was too dark to see who it belonged to. The girl took her by the arm and led her towards the light.

Reaching the end of the passageway, Tess could finally see her guide's shape. But the girl's face and figure were disguised by a floor-length hooded cloak.

The hooded figure touched the wall and it swung open, revealing two slight girls kneeling in front of a circle of candles. Arden and Meg, their faces daubed with cryptic symbols, continued their chanting, weaving back and forth as if possessed.

Tess was suddenly gripped by a fear that shot through her veins like iced lightning. Her heart thundered in her chest and she would have screamed if her voice hadn't caught in her throat.

What frightened Tess was not the eerie candlelight dancing over Arden and Meg's ghoulish faces. It wasn't even their strange chant.

What frightened Tess was the lone figure standing in the far corner of the room. She couldn't tell if the dark shadow was a man or a woman. All she knew was that it seemed to radiate waves of pure evil. And it terrified her to the very centre of her soul...

Chapter Five

*T*ess tried to stand, but her body was a mass of quivering jelly. The memory of the party had shaken her to the core.

"The police are leaving," Kelly whispered from the door. "Now you can go and talk to Mom and Dad."

Tess's heart was still pounding. She put her hand over her chest. "Kelly, something bad. Really bad..." Tess couldn't find the words to describe what she'd just seen in her head. "I can't talk right now."

"You don't have to." Kelly grabbed Tess's hand and pulled her into the hall. "Just let them see you."

"Not like this," Tess said, as they passed the upstairs bathroom. "I have to clean up. I don't want scare them any more than they already are." She pulled Kelly inside and shut the door.

The bathroom, with its clawfoot tub and pedestal sink, dated from the turn of the century when the old farmhouse was built. The window was hung with white eyelet curtains and looked out over the front of the house. Tess pushed aside one of the curtain panels to make sure the police had left.

The patrol car was gone, but in its place was a black sedan with tinted windows.

Tess motioned Kelly to the window. "Do you know that car?"

Kelly looked out. "No." She grabbed Tess's arm and pulled her. "Hurry up and wash your face."

"Wait!" The back electric window of the car lowered and Tess was certain she saw something glowing red inside. Before she could tell Kelly, the window slid shut again.

Adrenalin surged through her body. "Kelly," she gasped. "Something is after me. I feel it."

"Oh, Tess, now you're just being paranoid. That car could be some unmarked police car."

"It's not," she whispered, peering out through the curtain again. "I know it."

"Well, let's go talk to Mom and Dad.

They'll know what to do."

Tess quickly splashed water on her face. She had to think fast. She caught her breath when she saw her reflection in the mirror. She looked worse then she expected. Dark circles ringed her eyes, partly from stress and lack of sleep, and partly because her mascara had smeared during the night.

"Oh, Kelly, this is terrible." Tess leaned on the sink, watching the water swirl down the drain. "I can't stay. I have to get out. Now."

"What? Don't talk stupid."

Tess's heart was thudding in her chest as she shut the bathroom door and leant against it, blocking Kelly's way. "Kelly, its hard to explain because I don't understand it myself. But I know if I stay here even another hour, all of our lives will be in danger."

"Is it because of that car?"

Tess jerked her head up and down. "Someone in that car knows I'm here. I could feel their eyes looking at me."

Kelly frowned. "But you were behind the curtain..."

"It doesn't matter. I felt their eyes, burning through me."

Kelly's eyes widened. "Don't talk like that. You're scaring me."

"You think you're scared. I'm petrified. I don't have much time." Tess opened the bathroom door and raced toward the attic stairs, with Kelly right on her heels.

She peeled off what remained of her tattered costume and jammed it into her sister's arms. "Hold that for me."

"What are you going to do?" Kelly asked.

"Hide." Tess threw open the drawers of her antique chest of drawers and removed a dark purple turtleneck, jeans, underwear and wool socks. "Until I figure out what happened last night."

"Are you out of your mind?" Kelly hissed. "Where are you going to hide?"

Tess yanked on some clothes and grabbed a hairbrush from her dressing table. "I'm not sure." She tugged the brush through her hair, wincing at the mass of tangles it had become. "Now listen, show Mom and Dad my costume. That will prove I was here," she instructed, wrapping an elastic band round her hair.

"But you can't leave," Kelly protested. "You just got home!"

"Just do what I say!" Tess ordered impatiently.

From the top shelf of her wardrobe, she knocked down an overnight bag. Within seconds she'd shoved in gloves, a notepad and pen, her hairbrush, sunglasses, all of the contents of her piggy bank, a sweater, extra underwear and socks.

"Tess, I think that gouge over your eye is affecting your thinking," Kelly said.

"You may be right," Tess said, slipping her feet into her Doc Martens and shrugging on a fleece-lined jean jacket. "That's probably why I can't remember all that happened."

"But if you can't remember, why are you so certain you're in danger?"

"I just know it!" Tess hissed. "Look, I think Anthony's death is connected to that witches' ceremony I walked in on last night." Tess put her hands on her hips. "Tell me that Mom and Dad are going to buy that story."

"Well..."

"When I tell Mom I know my life is in danger, she'll tell me to lie down and take a nap."

"That's true," Kelly conceded. "But you

probably could use one, you look like hell."

Tess hurried out of her bedroom and down the stairs. "Just give me a head start before you talk to them," she whispered over her shoulder. "I promise to call and check in."

Tears filled her sister's eyes. "I don't know what to do. I shouldn't let you go like this. I mean, how long are you going to be gone? Overnight?"

"Of course not," Tess bluffed, not having thought that far ahead herself. "I'm just going to do a little sniffing round. When I find out what happened, I'll come right home."

Kelly's chin started to quiver. "While you're out playing Sherlock Holmes, I'm stuck here with the Mom and Dad freak-out! It's not fair."

Tess faced her sister. "Come on, Kelly. It will be OK. Just don't let anyone into the house. And keep a look out for that black car."

Kelly was trying to act brave, but she couldn't stop herself from weeping. "I'm worried about you," she said between sobs. "I can't stand the thought of something bad happening to you."

Tess held out her arms and hugged Kelly

hard. "I'm sorry to dump this on you," Tess said softly. "But I know in my heart of hearts that I have to leave." Gently she broke the embrace. "I'd better be going."

She moved to peer out the window in the bathroom. The dark sedan was still idling below. "I'll have to go out of your window and through the back woods," she whispered.

Before she left, Tess wrote a quick note at Kelly's desk, which Kelly promised to deliver after giving Tess a twenty minute head start. The note read:

Dear Mom and Dad,

Please don't worry. I'm OK. I know the police are looking for me, so I need to lie low until this is settled. Please believe me, I had nothing to do with the fire or the murder at the mansion. But I think I can find out who did. I love you and Kelly so much! Please trust in me.

Your loving daughter,
Tess

With a baseball cap pulled over her hair, Tess scurried through the woods behind her house. Normally, a walk through the area brought her peace. This morning, the woods were a tangle of exposed roots ready to trip her and sharp branches that scratched her face.

She came out of the woods a half mile from her house. She was not far from Ryan's house. But getting there without being seen was not going to be easy.

The town was going about its Saturday routine. Families were driving to and from music and dance lessons. Homeowners were raking dried brown leaves off their yards. Dogs were being taken out for walks. But something just didn't feel right.

Dark clouds had rolled in since dawn, leaving Brookston shrouded in grey. From every porch leered jack-o'-lanterns. Their jagged, toothy grins seemed to be mocking Tess.

At the corner of Ryan's block, Tess slipped into the Daylight Donuts shop. Keeping her head down, she made a beeline for the pay phone at the back, near the restrooms. Keeping her face turned to the wall, she dialed Ryan's number.

"Hello?" It was Ryan who answered. His voice carried an urgent tone.

"Are you alone?" Tess whispered, cupping her hand round the receiver.

"Tess? My god! Is that you?" Ryan asked.

"Answer me," she insisted. "Are you alone? Say yes or no – or I'll hang up."

"Yes," Ryan answered. "Tess, this is you, isn't it?"

"Are you surprised to hear from me?" she asked, thinking that there might be a distant chance that he could be in on this weird business, too.

"God, Tess, I'm so glad you're alive." His voice rang with what sounded like real sincerity. "I stayed at the mansion for hours, searching for you. I only went home when the police ordered everyone away. I've been sick with worry."

Hearing this made Tess feel better. Still, she had to be careful. He could be trying to fool her. "Ryan, tell me where you were when the fire broke out"

"Don't you remember?" he asked.

She hesitated, not willing to give him the

advantage. "Of course," she lied, "but I want to hear it from you."

He paused for a moment, then said, "I feel so stupid, Tess. Like it was all my fault."

"What do you mean?"

"My stupid temper," he explained. "My jealousy. If I hadn't got so upset when I found you with Anthony, maybe none of this would have happened."

"Me with Anthony?" she repeated.

"Come on, Tess," said Ryan. "Quit testing me! I said I was sorry!"

From the front of the restaurant, the huge, round woman behind the counter called, "A dozen bear claws, three jam doughnuts and two chocolate éclairs. Harold, your order is ready!"

"Where are you?" Ryan asked, suspiciously.

"At home," Tess fibbed. "That's the, um, TV in the background." Tess leant her forehead against the wall. "Listen, Ryan, I'm missing a few details about last night. Could you please tell me what happened?"

"Well," he began, "it wasn't long after we arrived when those jerks started to flirt with you."

"What jerks?" she repeated.

"Some guys from the team," he said. "They started whistling at your outfit – and I lost it. I pushed one guy to the ground. Then you ordered me out of the room."

"I did?" Tess asked.

"Then you got a glass of punch and went off to be with Rose."

Tess closed her eyes. "That's right. I was talking to Rose when Anthony came in. He was angry and yelled at his brother, Ian."

"I don't remember that," Ryan said. "I was at the food table."

"Then for some reason I went upstairs," she murmured. "And that's when things got bizarre."

The images swirled. Tess was back in the ballroom, standing near the refreshment table. Someone had slipped a note to her while she was dancing. Its message was simple, intriguing: *Meet me in the library. Come alone.*

Tess couldn't stand it. She had to know who it was from. She set her punch glass on a side table and fought her way through the crowd on the stairs.

"Foxy outfit," a guy in a werewolf mask rumbled, slipping his arms round Tess's waist. "Maybe you'd like to put a spell on me."

Even with the mask, Tess recognized Kurt Boharsky, one of Ryan's pals from the football team. She gave him an extra hard shove. "Lay off, Kurt."

"Hey, lighten up," Kurt protested as he backed off. "It's a party, for chrissake."

The first floor had a completely different feel to it from the rest of the mansion. The wall sconces along the long hall glowed dimly, giving a soft glow to the antique tables laden with vases of flowers. With the exception of one couple partially hidden behind a marble statue in an alcove, the floor seemed deserted.

She moved slowly down the hall, trying the doors to the rooms on either side. They were locked. Finally she found one that turned. She opened it, slowly.

"Hello," Tess called, timidly. "Anybody here?"

The room was dark and empty. Light from the hall played across the rows of bookshelves lining the walls, the heavy leather volumes gleaming dully in the half-light. She shut the door behind her and felt for the light switch on the wall. But when she flicked it, nothing happened. The room remained lit only by the light from outside the large, draped windows. And two candles on the mantelpiece.

Tess moved towards the light. She heard a movement behind her and, looking up at the gilt-edged mirror above the mantel, saw her own face, flushed from dancing.

"You look beautiful tonight," a voice intoned in a light accent.

Tess spun and found herself face to face with the tall blond in a red satin cape. "Anthony! I didn't see you come in."

"It is funny." The corners of his mouth curled up in a half-smile. "I never realized until this evening just how exquisite you were."

Tess chuckled. "What is this – a joke?"

Anthony took a step towards her, his piercing blue eyes focused intently on hers. "Do I look like I'm joking?"

Tess swallowed hard. She'd always considered Anthony very attractive and now that she was all alone with him, in this extremely romantic setting, she was finding him very hard to resist. "No," she murmured, as his head bent towards hers. "I guess not."

His lips had barely touched hers when the library door flew open, crashing against the wall.

"Back off, Stokes!" Ryan bellowed.

Anthony hardly flinched. He simply raised his head and turned.

The contrast was amazing. Anthony, slim and elegant in his tuxedo and red cape; and Ryan, thickly muscular and scruffy, in torn jeans and plaid flannel shirt. Ryan flew at Anthony with fists swinging. Anthony deflected one punch with the wave of his left arm. Then quick as lightning his right arm shot out and caught Ryan by the throat.

Ryan's face was twisted with pain and hatred. He gasped and clutched wildly at Anthony's hand. Anthony concentrated all of his energy on Ryan, who slowly collapsed to the floor.

"Anthony!" Tess shouted, as she watched Ryan struggling for air. "Let go of him."

Anthony's head jerked to the side. His pupils were dilated. He studied Tess for one second, as if trying to comprehend what she had just said. Then he released Ryan, who crumpled to the floor, gasping.

Tess was horrified at what had just occurred.

Ian appeared at the door, he was breathing excitedly. "They're here."

"Good. I'm ready for them." Anthony turned to Tess, as if Ryan weren't even in the room, and smiled. "I'll see you later."

"Everything was weird," Ryan's voice cut through her memory. "There I was lying on the floor, and Ian was at the door – and then something flew in the window."

"What was it?" Tess asked.

"I'm not sure. It looked like a—"

Tess caught her breath. "It looked like a what?"

But Ryan didn't answer her. The line had gone dead.

CHAPTER SIX

"*R*yan?" Tess called into the humming receiver. "Ryan, are you there?"

She banged the phone several times against the wall in frustration.

"Excuse me, are you having a problem?" a voice murmured close to her ear.

"Yikes!" Tess would have hurled the receiver in the air if it hadn't been attached by a metal cord to the phone. She spun and flattened herself against the wall. Directly in front of her, the collar of his now familiar black leather jacket flipped up round his neck, was Sebastian.

"Do you need a quarter?" he asked, an amused smile on his lips.

Tess blinked at him. "How did you get here?"

"The girl at the counter invited me in,"

Sebastian replied. "They're giving out samples of their glazed doughnuts."

"But how did you know I was here?" Tess gestured to her change of clothes and the baseball cap pulled low on her head. "I mean, how did you recognize me?"

"Nothing can disguise your beauty," Sebastian said, without a trace of sarcasm.

Tess flushed. She felt both delighted and a bit disconcerted by his directness. She hung up the receiver, realizing she'd have to talk to Ryan later.

"Have you had breakfast?" Sebastian asked.

Tess needed a moment to remember. "Actually, no."

"Well, try one of these." He reached into the paper bag and handed her a glazed jam doughnut. "Can't have you beating up phones on an empty stomach."

Tess took the doughnut and studied Sebastian. "Did you know I was in here?" she asked. "Be honest."

"Honestly?" he said without blinking. "Yes." Sebastian gestured to the dining area of the small doughnut shop. "Let me buy you a cup of coffee to go with that, and you can hear my confession."

Tess slipped her bag with all of her belongings over her shoulder and followed Sebastian back into the diner. She suggested they take a booth in the far corner. She still didn't want to be recognized by any townspeople.

Sebastian bought them two coffees and sat down. "When we said goodbye in the park, I was all set on going home. But – and please don't be offended – I couldn't get you out of my mind."

"Right. It's not every day you meet a weird barefoot girl who's up a tree in a cemetery," Tess joked.

"OK, the way we met *was* bizarre," he conceded. "But I still think fate brought us together."

"Sebastian, you sound like you've read one too many romances," she said, uncomfortable with his sincerity.

"Will you let me finish?" he said, gently touching her hand.

Tess shut up instantly.

"I went inside that restaurant, the Pewter Platter, and looked up your address in the phone book."

"You looked up my address?" Tess asked. She could have sworn she hadn't told him her last name. *Maybe I did and forgot. There are so many things I can't remember right now...*

"I wasn't going to let you simply disappear from my life," Sebastian continued. "I wanted to at least make sure you'd got home all right. Then when I drove by your place, I saw a ladder against the house at the back and a black car with its engine running parked in front."

"You saw the car, too?" Tess murmured. "Did it seem odd to you?"

"Except for the tinted windows, the car didn't seem odd," Sebastian replied, studying the liquid in his coffee cup. "What was odd was the sight of you climbing down the ladder and running like a frightened rabbit into the woods."

Tess set down her cup. "I wonder if anyone else saw me."

"I was quite alone," Sebastian assured her. "But I was worried about you, so..."

"You followed me here?" she concluded.

He cocked his head and nodded slowly.

"Now tell me honestly, *are* you all right?"

"The doughnut helps," she said, avoiding a direct answer. Tess stopped to dab a bit of jelly from her upper lip with a paper napkin.

"Will you tell me where you're going?" Sebastian asked, tossing his coffee cup in the trashcan near their table. Tess realized she hadn't noticed him drinking it, or even eating one doughnut. She decided she must have devoured them all. *Boy, I must have been starved.*

Sebastian now stood next to the table. "Can I take you somewhere?"

Tess stood up and tossed her napkin in the trash. Her plan had been to go see Ryan. But the phone call was so odd, and the look of pure hatred on Ryan's face last night still frightened her. He hadn't even bothered to ask where she'd been all night or how she got home. *No, I'm not going to Ryan's. Not now.*

"I was planning to visit my friend, Rose," Tess said suddenly. *Rose will help me sort things out.*

"Come on," Sebastian said, interrupting her thoughts. "I'll walk you out."

But no sooner had they stepped out the front

door of the doughnut shop when the black sedan cruised into view round the corner.

"There's that strange car again," Tess whispered, ducking back into the doorway. "The one that was at my house."

"We can slip out the back," Sebastian said, taking her arm.

In the alley behind the doughnut shop, Tess and Sebastian kept close to the wall, in case the car came by again.

"I'm not always this weird," said Tess weakly. "It's just that I don't know who that car belongs to. I don't know why it's following me."

They waited for a minute or two. Then Sebastian went out for a look, leaving Tess alone.

Sebastian is so considerate, she thought. *But should I trust him?* He certainly hadn't suggested or done anything improper since Tess had met him earlier that morning. *Give him a chance. Since he wasn't at the party, he's probably the only one you can trust.*

When Sebastian returned, he said, "The coast is clear. Can I drop you off somewhere?"

"With that car out there, I think I feel safer

on foot," replied Tess.

They left the alley and began walking west. Rose lived on the opposite side of town in one of the newer subdivisions. It took about fifteen minutes to get there, but Tess didn't mind. The walk gave her time to clear her head. And, though she felt guilty admitting it, she really was enjoying spending time with Sebastian.

"That's Rose's house." Tess pointed towards a row of houses that at first glance seemed exactly alike. Only the colours were different. Rose's home was a pale pink, while those on either side were lemon and pale green. The porches had tiny variations in their railings, and the garages alternated sides, but otherwise the houses looked as if they'd been stamped out with a cookie cutter.

"Hers is the pink one. Naturally." Tess giggled. "It goes with her name."

Sebastian smiled warmly. "It's good to hear you laugh."

"Hey, I'm a Taurus. As a rule we laugh a lot." Tess put a hand to her mouth. "But you may not be into that sort of thing."

"Oh, I dabble a little in astrology," he said, with a smile. "Let me see...I know your ruling planet is Venus. And that Taureans are usually loving and giving, but can also be very possessive, about people and things."

Tess thought about her porcelain collections and all of the other little prized objects she guarded so carefully in her room. "I think that's true," she admitted.

Before Tess could ask Sebastian his sign, the front door of the pink house opened. "There's Rose. She's with – oh, geez." Tess grabbed Sebastian by the arm and pulled him behind the neighbour's hedge. "Duck."

Sebastian, looking very befuddled, did as he was told. "Did you see the car again."

"No," Tess murmured, peering at the house through the thick hedge. "Something maybe even worse. Arden."

She was wearing an ankle-length black coat and carried something in her arms. Material. A deep red dress with black trim.

"Look at that," Tess muttered. "Arden is holding my dress. I lent it to Rose for homecoming."

"Arden." Sebastian repeated her name carefully. "She wouldn't be the girl you were telling me about, would she?"

Tess nodded firmly. "The witch." She ducked her head, embarrassed. "Or at least that's what she tells people."

"Is she friends with Rose?"

Tess sat back on her heels and tugged at the brim of her baseball cap. "No. They barely speak. Arden and her friends even put a hex on Rose once, at the school assembly. She was giving a speech and her index cards just flew out of her hands."

Sebastian raised one eyebrow. "Are you sure about this?"

Tess shrugged. "I only know what I saw, and what Rose told me later. She said it felt like something ripped them out of her hands. When she knelt to pick them up, Rose caught Arden sitting in the front row, laughing."

"This is some high school," Sebastian commented, rubbing his chin.

"Makes you want to go home and talk your parents into moving, huh?" Tess said, bending forward to peer through the hedge. "Oh, look, Arden is leaving. With *my* dress. And she's— oh, gross! She's hugging Rose!"

"Maybe Rose is one of *them*," Sebastian suggested.

"Oh, god, I hope not," Tess muttered, her eyes getting huge.

Arden hurried down the sidewalk in the opposite direction. She clutched the dress to her chest as she walked, and Tess could see her lips moving.

Tess crossed the fingers on both hands. "Please, please, don't let Arden put some kind of spell on me," she murmured, squeezing her eyes shut. "That's all I need."

Sebastian was still kneeling next to her. "Tess, don't be angry with me," he said, "but don't you think that Halloween may be going to everyone's head? I mean, all this talk of witches and spells is a little extreme."

Tess opened her eyes. "I sound like a total idiot, I know. You may be right. But ever since last night, I haven't felt like myself."

"What happened last night?" Sebastian prodded, gently.

But Tess was too agitated to answer.

"I can't stand it," she declared. "I'm going to talk to Rose. Supposedly she's my best friend. I have to find out what she's doing with Arden."

Tess grabbed her pack and, hopping over

the hedge, bolted across the street. "Rose, wait!"

Rose was just going inside her house when she heard Tess's voice. She turned and looked behind her. Her face went absolutely white.

"Tess? Is that really you?" she asked in a little girl's voice.

Tess leapt up the front steps and grabbed Rose by the shoulders. "Rose, what were you doing with Arden?"

"You're alive!" Rose cried, throwing her arms round Tess. "Oh, Tess, I was so worried!"

Tess untangled herself from Rose's embrace. "Answer me. Why did you give her my dress?"

Rose was stunned at the roughness in Tess's voice. She backed up, frowning. "Don't bark at me like that. She came by to help, Tess. She said she could find you."

Tess saw the hurt on her friend's face. She took a deep breath and softened her tone. "I'm sorry, Rose, but whatever happened last night isn't over. And I have to be careful. Now tell me why she has my dress."

Rose looked down at the porch. "I know I shouldn't trust Arden, but I was desperate to

90

find you. She said she needed a belonging of yours to call up your spirit."

"Is that what she told you?" Tess exclaimed. "Rose, how could you be so gullible? Arden probably wants to use it to cast a spell on me. To prevent me from finding out what really happened last night."

"I-I wasn't thinking," Rose stammered, putting both hands to her face. "I was so upset when they reported you missing, I thought you might be—" Rose burst into tears.

"Now don't cry," Tess said, wrapping her arm round Rose's shoulder. "It's OK. I'm all right, Tess. How could you know?" She hugged her friend. "But this is a lot more serious than anyone thinks. Has anyone else contacted you?"

"Well, the police questioned everyone who was at the party," Rose said, with a loud sniff. She wiped at her nose with the back of her hand. "I couldn't help them much. I was downstairs when the fire broke out," Rose said. "The next thing I knew people were screaming 'Fire! Fire!' and I didn't know where you were. I tried to get upstairs—"

"Ryan hasn't called you?" Tess cut in.

"No."

"Anyone from Anthony's family?"

Rose shook her head and sniffled once more. "Can you believe he's dead? It's all too incredible."

The mention of Anthony and the murder sent goose bumps up Tess's arms. She suddenly felt vulnerable out in the open. "Could we go inside?" she asked. "I need to think."

Rose pushed open the door. "Come on in, my parents aren't here. They've taken Grandma shopping."

Tess suddenly put her hands to her face. "Oh, I nearly forgot. I want you to meet my new friend." She cupped her hands round her mouth and shouted towards the hedge, "Sebastian. You can come out!"

"Who's Sebastian?" Rose asked, following Tess's gaze. The hedge stood silent and unmoving.

"Sebastian?" Tess called, a little more timidly. She dropped her hands to her side. "That's strange. I didn't see him leave."

Rose looked at Tess sceptically. "Tess, a lot of kids were hospitalized for smoke inhalation," she said. "I hear it can do strange things to your head."

Tess rolled her eyes. "Rose, I didn't make him up. For some reason he just disappeared. But he seems to do that. I think he's kind of shy. I'll explain it once we're inside."

Thunk.

The odd sound caught both girls by surprise. They froze. "Did you hear that?" Tess mouthed to Rose.

Rose nodded and pointed towards the side of the house. "It came from there," she mouthed back.

Tess gestured for Rose to stay put. Then she tiptoed as quietly as she could along the side of the house. As she rounded the corner she caught sight of a blonde girl in a tattered costume scaling the back yard fence.

"Stop!" Tess shouted, but the girl kept climbing.

Tess rushed to the fence and caught hold of the girl's ankle.

Hisss! The sound that came out of the girl didn't even sound human. She spun, her lips curled back like a wild animal, ready to bite.

"Carly!" Tess gasped, instantly letting go of

her foot.

The look on Carly's face was frightening. Hardly human. But what was really terrifying were her eyes – they were yellow, like a cat's, with vertical pupils.

CHAPTER SEVEN

*T*he sight of Carly's face, fierce and cat-like, had completely unnerved Tess. She scrambled as fast as her legs could carry her back to the front porch, where she grabbed Rose and yanked her into the house.

The girls pressed against the living room wall, peeking out through the picture window's drapes.

"Carly was at the fence," Tess huffed, out of breath. "Something horrible's happened to her. She looks..."

"What?" Rose asked. "Tell me."

Tess shook her head. "I don't know, it was her eyes, she didn't look...human." Tess peered cautiously out the window again. She leant her head back against the wall. "Oh, god, Rose, I am *really* scared."

"Tess, you have to tell me what's going on,"

Rose said, snapping the drapes shut. "Right now."

Tess slumped to the floor next to the curtain, keeping her back against the wall. She quickly retold the events of that morning, from waking up in the alley, unable to remember how she got there or anything about the night before, to seeing the black sedan with the tinted windows. "That car was at my house this morning. And it followed me to Daylight Donuts, where I phoned Ryan."

"How is he handling this?" Rose asked. "He was very shook up last night. Ryan was one of the kids they had to treat for smoke inhalation."

"I didn't get a chance to talk to him for long," Tess explained. "We were cut off. I think my quarter ran out, which is weird – but then *everything* that's happened to me has been weird."

Rose sat on the floor on the other side of the window, hugging her knees to her chest. "Tess, last night when the fire broke out, I tried to find you," she said. "My mind's a little jumbled, but I remember fighting my way through the kids on the stairs. Everyone was screaming and trying to get to the front door."

"How did you know I was upstairs?"

"You got that note, remember? Telling you to go to the library."

Tess nodded. "How long was it between the time that I left and the fire?"

Rose pursed her lips. "About thirty or forty minutes. I know because I danced to several songs, and I was just about to get another glass of punch when someone screamed that there was a fire."

"What did you see upstairs?" Tess asked.

"People in costume, running. But the flames weren't coming from the library. They were in another room. Towards the end of the hall." I thought I heard your voice scream, 'Oh my god! Get away!' and I ran to find you."

Rose put her head in her hands as the memory flooded back. "Smoke was everywhere," she continued, "but I covered my mouth with the hem of my skirt and ran forward. You were screaming and screaming."

Tess felt her throat, feeling the small wound under her ear. "That's why my throat felt so sore and scratchy this morning."

"When I reached the door to that last room,

it was filled with flames. But behind the flames were three figures."

"Arden, Meg and Carly," Tess murmured.

"No." Rose raised her head. Her eyes were red-rimmed. "I don't even remember seeing them. There were two boys – I think Anthony was one – but I couldn't see the other boy's face."

"Who was the third person?" Tess asked.

"You, Tess." Rose stared at her friend. "You."

Tess felt her pulse quicken. "What was I doing?" she asked, her voice barely above a whisper.

"Protecting yourself with something. You held it in front of you like a shield." Rose put her head back on her knees. "Then the flames and smoke got so bad I had to run. I couldn't save you." Rose started to sob, making little hiccup sounds. "I've felt so guilty because I didn't help you."

Tess crawled across the floor and put her arm round Rose's shoulders. "But Rose, there was nothing you could do. And I made it out. It's OK."

Rose continued to weep. "When they

couldn't find your body, I was frantic. I called Arden. I told her I'd do anything if she'd just help me find you."

"I see." Tess nodded slowly. "So that's how Arden wound up at your house."

Rose raised her tear-streaked face. "Now I'm afraid I've only made matters worse. Arden has your dress. Who knows what terrible thing she'll do?"

"Rose, don't cry." Tess patted Rose gently on the back. "Really. Arden is a problem but we can deal with it. We can go to her house, and steal the dress back if we have to. There's something else that worries me."

Rose wiped her eyes with her fingertips. "What?"

A distant rumbling interrupted Tess's thoughts. She put a finger to her lips, then carefully felt for a fold in the drapes.

The black car was there, just as she suspected. She listened to the engine idle, then heard the sound of a power window being lowered. Tess held her breath.

A moment passed. It felt like an hour.

Then the sedan moved on.

Tess and Rose breathed a sigh of relief.

"That car," Tess muttered. "I wish I knew who was inside. I have a feeling, if I could find that out, a huge part of this mystery would be solved."

Rose tugged at the three tiny crosses piercing her left ear. "Have you talked to your parents, Tess? Maybe this is just too much for you to handle."

"My parents!" Tess leapt to her feet and hurried into Rose's kitchen. "I have to call them, to let them know I'm OK."

She grabbed the portable and took it with her to check the back windows. "Rose, please keep watch out of that window for any movement of any kind."

Rose nodded. "I know, I'm supposed to watch for Meg."

"Watch for Meg and any other unusual creatures," Tess said, punching in her numbers. "Like a cat. With yellow eyes."

"Langleys'." It was Kelly who answered the phone.

"Kelly, it's me," Tess said. "Keep calm. Pretend one of your goofy friends is calling. Don't alert Mom or Dad that it's me, or I'll hang up. Understand?"

"What do you think I am – stupid or something?" Kelly said in a low voice.

Tess overlooked the opportunity to say something sarcastic. "I'm at Rose's. But I don't think I can stay here for long. That black car has followed me."

"How did it find you?"

"I don't know," Tess said, grabbing an apple from the fruit bowl on the kitchen counter. "It just did. It's like it has radar. How did Mom and Dad take the note?"

"How do you think?" Kelly's voice was barely audible. "They were relieved at first. Then they got furious. They can't believe you'd run away like this. Dad's been out cruising the streets in the car, looking for you. I'm surprised he's not over there right now."

"What?" Tess hurried back to the living room and covered the mouthpiece with her hand. "My dad's out looking for me," she told Rose. "If he pulls up in front, shout."

"Tess, something else weird happened," Kelly whispered.

"What? Is everyone all right?"

"Yes, yes. It's just that shortly after that black car drove away, that geek brother of

101

Anthony's showed up at our door."

"What did he want?"

"Well, he asked if we'd heard from you," Kelly reported. "I told him we hadn't. I said Mom and Dad were crazy with worry, but that I was looking forward to taking over your room if you didn't show up soon."

"Very funny," Tess said. "Sounds like Ian figures I'm still alive." She picked up a pencil and wrote: WHO KNOWS I'M ALIVE? on the message pad. Then she wrote: IAN, CARLY, ROSE, RYAN. Then as an after thought she wrote: MOM, DAD, KELLY, SEBASTIAN.

"Oh, and I told him I was really sorry to hear about his brother. Then Ian shrugged and said, 'Why? I'm not.'"

"You're kidding!" Tess gasped.

"What?" Rose ran to press her head next to the receiver. "I want to hear."

"Ian said he was sorry Anthony got fried," Kelly continued, "but that he was tired of standing in his shadow. Now it was his turn to shine."

Tess shuddered. "What an insensitive creep."

"Creep is right," Kelly said. "The guy is now number one suspect on my list of murderers."

Tess nodded. "If what you say is true, maybe he killed Anthony out of jealousy."

"But if he thinks killing his brother is suddenly going to make him handsome, he should try looking in the mirror," Kelly said. "The guy gives ugly a bad name."

Tess took a crunchy bite of her apple and the noise seemed unnaturally loud in her ears. "But if he killed Anthony, why would he want to talk to me?"

Rose pulled her head away from the receiver. "Maybe you saw him do it, and he wants to get rid of you."

Tess took Rose's deduction calmly. She had spent the morning with so much adrenaline pumping through her that she'd started to become numb. "You may be right there."

"He did mention something about a book," Kelly said. "One that he thought you had."

"A library book?" Tess asked, incredulous. "I can't imagine that Ian and I have the same taste in books. I don't even think he can read."

"Not a library book," Kelly said. "He kept calling it The Book. You know how Aunt

103

Dorsie always says 'the Good Book' when she really means the Bible? Well, he used 'The Book' in the same way."

"Ian wants a Bible?" Rose was totally confused.

"No!" Kelly was starting to shout. "Not a Bible. It was some leather-bound thing that was big and old. And he said he wanted it back. He even said he'd give me one dollar if I would hunt for it and call him. Can you believe that cheapskate? One dollar! I can barely buy a Coke and a candy bar with that."

"Kelly," Tess warned. "Lower your voice. Mom might hear you."

"Mom just went out to the garage. Dad's back, and it's her turn to go and look for you."

Tess drew a heart on the notepad. "Look, Kell, tell them I called in to say I was fine. I'll call back in a few hours. Tell them to please stop looking for me!"

She said goodbye, then flicked the off switch on the phone. Tess tore the note off the pad and jammed it in the pocket of her jeans. "I have to get out of here," she told Rose. "Mom's in the car and will probably be coming by any minute."

"OK, I'll go with you." Rose raced to grab her coat.

Tess watched her for a second. "Rose, can I borrow one of your brother's jackets? It doesn't matter if it's an old one. I need to be in disguise."

Rose frowned. "Sure. Check upstairs, I'm sure Brian's got something."

Moments later Tess was stepping over the clutter of wrinkled clothes and sports equipment strewn across the floor of Brian's room. "Geez, it's like an obstacle course in here."

"Brian says this prevents sneak attacks," Rose said, digging in the back of his closet and pulling out a dark-green down jacket with ski patches all over the arms. "Here. This should do it."

Tess slipped on the jacket and then exchanged her baseball cap for a maroon knitted watchman's cap. "Anyone watching for a jean jacket might miss me in this," she said as they hurried back down the stairs. At the back door Tess peered out carefully, scanning the back yard and bordering trees for any movement.

"Can we take your bikes?" she asked.

"Sure," Rose replied, hurrying to catch up with Tess, who was already half way to the garage. "But where are we going?

"Arden's." Tess swatted the cobwebs off Brian's ten-speed and looped her leg over the seat. "To get my dress. And to get some answers."

CHAPTER EIGHT

*Hot-headed Mars is transiting Aries, so watch
out for feisty tempers, either from you – or
others spewing hot lava at you. Don't play
with matches unless you have a fire
extinguisher handy.*

Arden lived in the oldest part of town, a few
streets beyond the high school. The girls
avoided the main streets, pedalling instead
along side streets and alleys. All the while Tess
kept a nervous watch for the black car and her
mother's silver minivan.

"What do you think that book business is all
about?" Rose asked as they rode along. "I
mean, I think it's very weird that the very
morning his brother dies, Ian is going door to
door searching for an old book."

"It must be a very important old book," Tess

said, pumping her legs as hard as she could.

"Worth a lot," Rose added.

My entire kingdom.

Tess squeezed the brakes and her bike skidded to a stop, spraying gravel in every direction. "What did you say?"

Rose swung her bike in a wide arc and circled back to Tess. She dragged her left foot and slowed to a stop. "I said, worth a lot."

"You didn't say anything else?" Tess leant over her handlebars and narrowed her eyes at Rose. "Like – my entire kingdom?"

"Of course not."

"I heard a voice," Tess confessed. "It was very clear." As she spoke, Tess could feel goose bumps creep up to the base of her hairline. She put her hand on Rose's handlebars. "Are you certain you didn't hear a thing?"

Rose's eyes grew very huge and frightened. "No, Tess, I swear," she whispered. "Maybe you were remembering something. And the memory was so strong that you heard the words spoken out loud."

"Maybe." Whatever she had heard had given Tess the distinct impression that she was being watched. She checked the houses on either side of the street, then searched the trees. Nothing. Finally she hopped back on her bike seat. "Rose, let's get out of here. We can take the short cut to Arden's."

They wheeled away, quickly getting up to full speed. Tess dug in with all her might, ducking her head low over the front wheel. The girls turned at the next corner.

Suddenly a gust of wind carrying swirls of orange and red leaves almost knocked them off their bikes.

"What the...?" began Tess. Then she noticed where they were.

Barkham Street.

It was the scariest street in town – and with good reason. More than a century before, a madwoman had chopped her parents into small pieces in the basement of her home on that street. Today the crime was the stuff of scary stories and tasteless jokes. Usually Tess thought they were funny, but not now. Not on Halloween. Definitely not in the wake of the horror at the Hawthorne Mansion.

"What's the idea, Rose?" Tess demanded. "This isn't the short cut. We missed it by two blocks. See?" She pointed to the opposite end of the street, where the faded brick walls and slate roof of a building were just visible above the trees. "The high school's over there."

"Look, Tess, I was only following you," Rose shot back.

"Great. Now we've got to go right past the old Hilford place to get to it. I hate that house. It gives me the creeps."

"So don't look at it when you go by," Rose said, reasonably. "Come on."

The girls pushed down hard on their bicycle pedals. Keeping their eyes glued on the road ahead, they tried not to look at the homes decorated for Halloween on either side of the street. Some had witches silhouetted on the doors. Others, black cats and ghosts painted on the windows. One front yard was filled with cardboard tombstones and plastic, life-size skeletons sitting on bales of dried hay. Another house had a bed-sheet ghost hanging from the bare limbs of a sycamore tree.

As they neared the crumbling Hilford place, Tess felt her mouth go dry with fear. The house hadn't been lived in for nearly a decade and looked ghastlier than ever.

"Come on, Tess," urged Rose, as they swept by. "Hurry!"

Tess allowed herself one look at the Hilford place. To her astonishment, a light was burning inside.

"Rose! Stop!" Tess shouted. She pointed to the light in the front window of the first floor.

The two girls stood in the street, peering up.

"I thought it had been abandoned for good," Rose said. "When old man Hilford died."

"I thought so, too," replied Tess. "Remember how weird he was supposed to be?"

Rose nodded. "He never moved from that recliner he kept by the window. I heard that when they found him dead, his body was surrounded by years and years of newspapers. Newspapers stacked high, with only a path to the bathroom and a path to the kitchen. Weird!"

"He didn't have any children," said Tess. "Right?"

"I don't know for sure," Rose said. "My mom once said the house passed to some distant relatives from Europe – but no one ever heard from them. You'd think the town would condemn the place and tear it down."

The discussion ended when the light inside started to move.

"Tess, let's get out of here!" Rose hissed.

"Wait!" Tess put her hand on Rose's arm and nodded towards the house.

The front door creaked open and a figure carrying an old hurricane lamp appeared on the rickety porch.

It was a man dressed in clothes from another time period. Black trousers. Long mourning coat. High-necked collar and black silk jabot. His hair was pulled into a ponytail at his neck and a stovepipe hat was perched on his head.

Tess shook her head, not believing the sight. "Do you see what I see?"

Rose nodded. "He looks like an undertaker out of a Dickens' story."

"Tonight's Halloween," Tess said in a shaky voice. "Maybe he's trying out his costume."

"But why would he be at the old Hilford place?" Rose asked.

"I don't know." Tess fumbled with her foot to get it back on her bike pedal. "And I don't want to know."

"Wait! Look who's with him."

A girl in a tattered black dress and wild hair appeared on the porch.

"Carly!" Tess breathed.

The moment the girl saw them on their bikes, she gasped and darted back inside.

"She just went to tell somebody about us," Tess croaked. "Let's get out of here."

The girls flew down the street as fast as their bikes would carry them. The high school went by in a blur and they were riding down the narrow gully bordering the playing fields. Out the corner of her eye, Tess caught a flash of movement and in an instant knew they weren't alone. Something was keeping pace with them, running through the brush and trees.

Just before the gully rose back up to street level, a black cat, with gleaming yellow eyes, sprang out of the bushes.

"Rose, look out!" Tess screamed.

Rose braked too suddenly and her bike skidded out from beneath her. "Aiiiee!" she screamed as she fell heavily on to the rough asphalt.

Tess hopped off, letting her bike crash on

the side of the gully. But someone else was at Rose's side ahead of her.

"Ian!" Tess gasped. "Where did you come from?"

"I've been following you," he huffed, out of breath. Maybe he had been the figure she'd seen darting through the brush. But where was the cat?

Rose, her face wrenched with pain, rocked back and forth, clutching her bleeding elbow. Blood poured from the scrape along her forearm. It was also oozing from a deep gash in her leg. "Oh, god, it hurts. It hurts."

"Do you think it's broken?" Tess asked, reaching out to feel her friend's arm.

But Ian was between them in a flash. His hand shot out and caught hold of Rose's arm. "If it's not broken now, it can be in half a second." Ian gave her arm a small twist and Rose screamed in pain.

Tess raised her hand to hit Ian, but he was surprisingly quick for such a lumpy person. He caught hold of her wrist, saying, "Ah-ah-ah! I wouldn't do that if I were you." He twisted Rose's wrist again. "Tell your friend – no hitting."

Rose squeezed her eyes shut in pain. "Tess!" she cried. "Back off. Please."

Tess wrenched her arm out of Ian's grasp. "What do you want?"

His dark, intense eyes seemed to bore a hole in her. His lips curled as Ian said, "The Book."

"Book?" Tess asked innocently.

"Don't play games!" stormed Ian. "This is bigger than you ever imagined. That fire at the mansion is only a taste of what could happen."

"So you admit you started the fire," Tess snapped.

"Me?" Ian threw back his head and laughed.

"How can you laugh?" Tess shouted. "Your own brother was killed in that fire."

Ian twisted Rose's wrist harder and she instantly whimpered, "Stop it. Oh, Ian, please."

"Tell your friend to give me The Book," Ian said, smoothing Rose's hair away from her face with his other hand. "And I'll let you go."

Rose shot Tess a pleading look, the pain clearly etched across her face. Tess pressed the heels of her hands into her eyes and murmured, "Book. Book. I'm trying to remember a book."

Ian dragged Rose with him as he inched his

face right under Tess's. "Richly tooled leather, with gold lettering," he whispered. "Thick. The Book is very thick. And heavy. Oh, so heavy. On the front cover, a five-pointed star."

As he spoke, the five-pointed star began to burn in Tess's memory. She could see it clearly, in a pentagram and glowing in the light...

Candlelight. Dozens of lit candles.

Arden and Meg were kneeling round a circle, their faces lit feverishly from the burning candles that formed a pattern on the floor. The room smelled of exotic incense and burning wax.

Arden's eyes looked heavy and drugged. A large leather book lay open in front of her. Meg and Arden chanted – a low guttural sound in a language Tess didn't understand.

A cloaked figure stood in the corner, barely visible. Carly?

Then she heard Carly's voice from behind her. "I've brought the offending party."

Arden raised her right hand, in which she clutched a tiny dagger. Its blade gleamed in the light, and Tess could see that the blade was inscribed with ornate designs. "The fire is lit. The ritual is begun."

Tess was frightened. If this was some sort of a party joke, it had gone too far. She wanted to run but couldn't – her legs felt like lead.

Meg and Arden continued their chanting. As they chanted, the figure in the corner seemed to fill the room. Its shadow grew larger and larger.

Suddenly the twin doors flew open. It looked like Anthony, filling the doorway. But Tess wasn't sure. His face, once serene and handsome, was twisted into a savage grimace. His blood-red lips curled back to reveal fierce, sharp teeth.

He trained his eyes, which once were blue but now seemed black and nearly sightless, on Arden. "Stop now, you fool! You don't know what you've done!"

A gust of cool breeze brought Tess back to the present. "The book," she murmured. "Arden had the book. Arden!"

Ian's nostrils flared and he released Rose's arm. "You liar. I saw you with it!"

Tess turned to run, but tripped over her bike.

Her hand was tangled in the spokes and, as she struggled to pull it free, Ian caught hold of her throat. "You'll tell me the truth, or I'll rip your throat out."

"Help!" Tess choked. "Somebody, help!"

Rose, who was sobbing and trying to pull Ian away from Tess, tried to scream too, but her voice caught in her throat.

Suddenly, out of nowhere, a girl leapt among them, snarling, clawing her hands in all directions.

"Oh my god," Rose gasped. "It's Carly."

Ian released Tess, and all three turned to stare at the pale intruder. Carly looked more like a large wildcat then a human. Her skin was mottled like a jaguar, her nails thick and curved like talons. She faced each one of them in turn, hissing, spitting, searching for her prey.

Then she attacked.

CHAPTER NINE

With one powerful leap, Carly flew over Tess and landed on Ian, knocking him to the ground.

"Help!" he screamed.

Carly tore at Ian with her tiger-like teeth, ripping into his flesh. He howled in pain, and somehow threw her off.

He dived forward and snatched up a tree limb lying at the edge of the gully. He swung it viciously at Carly, who caught the limb in her mouth. Her powerful jaws snapped it in two, leaving Ian holding a jagged stub in his hand.

"She's trying to save us," Tess rasped as she crawled to Rose's side. "Carly's trying to save us."

Then Ian lunged at Carly with the remaining part of the limb, striking Carly squarely between her shoulders.

She crumpled with an agonizing cry of pain. Showing no mercy, Ian leapt on her.

Rose struggled to get to her feet, unaware of the sweet-smelling fog drifting into the gully. But Tess saw it and felt it. It didn't frighten her. Quite the opposite. She felt comforted by it. "Rose, look," she whispered.

The fog lowered itself to the ground round Tess and Rose and crept to where Ian and Carly were fighting. Silently, the fog encircled Ian and worked its way up to his neck before he sensed it was there.

By then it was too late. Tendrils of fog coiled round his neck like a python. Ian's hands tore at his throat, his eyes bulged out. His skin turned blue, then a ghastly white. He sank out of sight into the swirling grey mist.

"Where is he?" Rose whimpered, burying her head in Tess's shoulder. "I can't see a thing."

"Mrrooow!" something yowled from within the swirling vapour. Then a scrawny black cat with yellow eyes darted past Rose and Tess. Seconds later they heard the dull thud of footsteps pounding away from them through the gully.

The fog seemed to have shrouded the entire neighbourhood. Tess could no longer make out the outline of the high school. But she could hear sounds coming from that direction. A screeching of car brakes. Voices carrying eerily across the parking lot.

"Hey, watch where you're going!"

"It's the fog – I can barely see my hand in front of my face. Must have rolled in from the ocean."

"It's a real pea-souper."

Tess, her arm round Rose, limped towards the voices. Rose's leg was bleeding badly and Ian had wrenched her arm hard enough to sprain it. "It's going to be OK, Rose," Tess murmured. "There are people at the school. Can't you hear them."

Rose nodded and whimpered, "I want to go home. I want my mom and dad."

The girls stumbled across the street into the school parking lot. The fog was starting to lift and just ahead Tess could make out a figure in black.

"Hello?" she called. "Please, could you please help us?"

The figure stepped forward through the

shifting clouds. "Tess?" a familiar voice called. "Is that you?"

Tess squinted. "Ryan?"

The boy moved closer. He was dressed in a black leather jacket and jeans. "No, it's Sebastian. Are you all right?"

Tess was so befuddled to see Sebastian at her school that she couldn't give a straight answer. "No, we've had a bike accident – what are you doing here? – the fog was confusing – and Ian, oh, he's disgusting..."

Sebastian hurried forward and looped his arm round Rose's waist to help support her. "Excuse my forwardness," he said, helping her through the parking lot.

"I guess you must be Sebastian," Rose said, trying hard not to wince at the pain. "I was starting to think Tess made you up."

"No," he replied. "I'm very real." He frowned at her leg. "And so's that wound. You'd better have a doctor look at that. There may be one inside the school."

The fog had now cleared to a thin mist and Tess could make out the shapes of several teens huddled round the back entrance. "What's going on? It's Saturday," Tess said, pausing behind a red pick-up in the parking lot. She wasn't sure she wanted to be seen by any students from school. They'd have too many questions and she still had no answers.

"Why are so many kids here on a Saturday?" she asked.

"Tonight's Halloween," Rose reminded her. "The Spanish Club is hosting a haunted house, remember?"

Tess cocked her head. "Then what are you doing here, Sebastian?"

"My family is moving into my uncle's house, just a few streets away," he explained. "I saw the parking lot was filled with cars, and figured this would be a good chance to check out the school. You know, get the lie of the land before I start on Monday."

Even though she was in pain, Rose recognized a cute boy when she saw one. "You're going to our school? That's great," she said, flashing a dazzling smile. "Maybe I can be your guide."

Tess couldn't believe the sharp feeling of jealousy that flared up inside her. "I'm showing Sebastian the school," she said, in a tone that told Rose to back off.

Rose blinked at Tess in surprise. "OK, Tess. That's fine." She winced and reached down to touch her leg. "I don't feel so good right now." She turned to Sebastian. "Why did you think there'd be doctors inside?"

"The police set up a temporary desk in the gym to gather information about last night's fire," he replied. "They've also brought in two grief counsellors to help students deal with Anthony Stokes's death."

"It wasn't just a death," Rose reminded Sebastian. "It was a murder. And I think I know who did it." She glanced back over her shoulder toward the gully and shuddered. "That evil little brother of his, Ian."

"What makes you so certain?" Sebastian asked.

"He tried to break my arm and threatened to rip out Tess's throat – all because of some stupid old book."

"Did he want to steal a book from you?" Sebastian asked.

Tess let out an exasperated, "Yes! Except I don't have his book. Arden does." She put her hands to her head and murmured slowly, "But it was never Ian's book in the first place.

It was—"

"Mine," Anthony hissed. "That book is mine, and I'll have it back."

"It's your own fault," Arden murmured. "You told me the *Book of Shadows* held all the secrets of the universe. Of course, I want to know those secrets, too."

"Arden," cooed Anthony, as if talking to a small child, "give me the grimoire. It does not belong to you. You could not possibly begin to know what to do with it. In your hands, there is great danger for all of us. Its power, if you misuse it, will return on you three times over. What you create – you will become. Remember, the evil that affects one thing affects all things."

Arden's face twitched, as if she was confused.

"Now give it back – before you call forth powers you'll never be able to stop." Anthony held out his hand, palm up.

Arden was about to step forward, when abruptly she changed her mind and rushed into the centre of the pentagram. Her skirt just brushing the top of the burning candles, she started to turn in a circle. She looked at Meg and Carly, and begged, "Tell me! What should I do?"

Before they could say anything, Anthony lunged at Arden, knocking over several candles in the process. He lunged desperately for the book. It flew out of her hands and skidded towards the back of the room.

The burning candles rolled across the uneven floor. One ignited the drapes, which instantly burst into flames. Another crashed against the wall, showering live sparks in a glowing arc.

A second river of fire, fuelled by the spilled wax and incense, ignited the wallpaper.

Meg rushed to help Arden, but the ragged hem of her witch's dress caught on fire. She screamed in panic, flailing with her hands at her burning dress.

Within seconds, the room was engulfed in flames and smoke.

Carly opened the door to the hall as Tess rushed to help Meg. Tess struck something with her foot. She stopped, reached down — and felt the book. She snatched it up and used it to beat out the flames riding up Meg's legs.

The smoke was so intense it was impossible to breathe.

"Get out!" Tess screamed. She pushed Meg through the open door and started to follow.

"Not so fast!"

Someone pulled her back, although Meg and Carly had escaped. Tess could hear them screaming in the hall, "Fire! Everybody, run!" And Rose's voice, calling, "Tess! My god, Tess, are you in there?"

"Tess?" Rose waved her hand in front of Tess's face. "Can you hear me?"

"I had the book," Tess murmured. "In my hands."

Rose waved her hand in front of Tess's face once more. "Hello? Tess, you're really freaking me out. Please answer. Can you hear me?"

Tess blinked several times, put her own hand up to block her eyes. "Yes! Quit swatting at me."

"I think we need to march right in there and talk to the police," Rose declared. "We'll go together. We can tell them all we know."

"I wouldn't do that if I were you." Sebastian

took a step sideways, blocking their way. His hands were thrust deep in his jacket pockets and, with his tall frame, he looked a little threatening.

"Why?" Rose asked, hopping backwards and clutching at Tess's arm.

"Why?" Sebastian repeated. "Because right now Tess is their number one suspect in last night's murder." He trained his deep brown eyes on Tess. "You walk in there now...and they'll arrest you."

"Oh, god, don't let them see me!" Tess pulled away from Rose and leapt back behind the truck. She peered round the side of the wheel and hissed, "Why didn't you tell me that right away?"

Sebastian stepped past Rose and knelt on one knee beside Tess. "Because I wasn't quite sure what to say," he murmured. "You see, you never told me you were at that party."

Tess put her head in her hands and confessed, "Well, I was. All right? But I can't remember what happened. Now weird cars are following me, Ian Stokes is threatening to hurt me because of a book, and the police want me for murder." Tess lifted her head, hoping she looked defiant, but her quivering chin gave her away. "Now you know everything!" she said through a flood of tears.

"Hey." Sebastian folded his arms round her and hugged her gently. "You don't need to cry."

"I can't help it," Tess sobbed, pressing her cheek into his shoulder. "I'm scared and confused, and I just can't think what to do."

Sebastian smoothed her hair back from her face. "Would you take my advice?"

Tess nodded, keeping her head pressed against his shoulder, not wanting him to release her. "Yes."

As he spoke, his lips brushed against her temple. "I think Rose should go inside and get some help with her leg and arm. And you need some rest. I could take you home. I have my car here."

Tess closed her eyes and murmured, "Rest. I'd like that."

He stroked her hair. "Your parents will know what's best to do. They'll talk to the police."

Tess could feel her muscles relax as she nodded in agreement. *I should never have tried*

129

to do this alone. He's right. Mom and Dad will help me. Tess pulled her head back and looked up at Sebastian. "Please. Take me home."

"Tess?" Rose called from the other side of the truck. "My leg is really bleeding. I've got to get help."

"Sebastian is going to help you inside the school, Rose," Tess said. "And then he's going to take me home."

"OK." Rose limped gingerly towards them along the side of the truck. "But be careful – and call me as soon as you get home."

Sebastian was still kneeling beside Tess. He took her by the shoulders and gazed at her with his deep, penetrating eyes. "Are you going to be all right?"

Tess nodded. "I think so. But hurry back."

He hesitated for a moment, then leant forward and kissed her.

The kiss was brief, but wonderful.

Tess closed her eyes. She wanted to savour the moment.

Sebastian moved his lips to her cheek and kissed her there. Then he moved to her neck. "You're hurt," he whispered, "just below your ear."

"I can't feel a thing," Tess murmured happily.

So Sebastian covered the wound gently with his lips. And Tess was happy, even if he pressed a bit too hard against her soft, vulnerable flesh.

CHAPTER TEN

You've got to confide in someone. Seek out a
friend while Venus is settling into Libra. Her
bright Venusian light will shine on your
enemies and smoke them out.

Tess watched Sebastian help Rose to the
school. He had insisted on walking on her right
side, saying that was his strong arm. Sebastian,
ever the gentleman, held the door and waited
until Rose gestured for him to come inside.
The glass door shut behind them and Tess
waited.

Her stomach growled and she realized it
was getting late in the afternoon. All she had
eaten that day was an apple, and that doughnut
round ten in the morning. That was when she'd
called Ryan.

Ryan!

Tess hadn't thought about him all day. How strange, after thinking about him constantly for nearly six months.

But then Ryan had disappeared. They'd gone to the party, he'd flown into a jealous rage – and that was that. He'd deserted her. Rose had come upstairs when the fire broke out. But not Ryan.

Now when she needed help the most, a perfect stranger was coming to her aid. It was hard to think of Sebastian as a stranger. She'd only known him for ten hours, but they'd already been through a lot together. *Or at least I have.*

Sebastian had promised to drive her home in his car. Tess inched out from behind the pick-up, wondering which car would be his.

"Kit Conroy's Subaru," she murmured, going down the line of cars. "Tom Wishengrad's Blazer. Or rather his dad's Blazer. And—"

Tess froze. *That car. The black one with the tinted windows.* It was in the next parking aisle. The engine was on, as usual, and all of the windows rolled up. *How did I miss seeing it before?*

The fog had obscured everything. But the sound of that engine? Its throaty rumble was unmistakable. Tess's heart sped up as if to match the engine's rhythm.

"I've got to run!" she gasped. "Hide."

The car faced the high school. Ducking as low as she could, Tess ran the opposite direction. She crossed two rows of cars on her hands and knees, until she reached the cement speed bumps at the edge of the parking lot. Then she leapt across the sidewalk into the street, making a beeline for the first house she recognized, a stately Victorian from the turn of the century.

The curtains were drawn, but Tess ran round the back. "She has to be home, " she murmured. "She told Rose she'd be here." Tess scurried across the cement patio, up the back porch steps, and pounded with both fists on the door.

"Arden! It's me, Tess. Open up!"

She beat on the door several more times. "Arden, I know you're in there!"

Tess pressed her ear to the door. She thought she heard movement inside, but she wasn't sure. Finally she heard the sound of the lock being undone. The door opened slightly, the chain still drawn, and a pair of wary, frightened eyes peered out at her.

"Tess? What are you doing here?"

"Let me in, and I'll tell you." Tess wasn't anxious to spend too much time out in the open.

"Are you alone?" Arden asked.

"No, I've brought the football team with me," Tess shot back sarcastically. "What do you think? Now let me in."

Arden shut the door and Tess could hear the rattle of the chain being undone. When the door opened again, Arden said, "Come in – but go straight to the basement. I don't want anyone to know I'm home. And don't turn on any lights!"

Tess hurried inside. It had been a long time since she'd been in Arden's house, but she still remembered the layout. Straight through the kitchen lay the dining and living rooms. Three bedrooms were upstairs, and the basement steps were just off the kitchen.

Tess felt her way down the darkened stairs to the basement laundry room, where a small lamp was lit. The windows above the washer and dryer had been covered with blankets and old bedspreads. She inched forward into the den, which was really just a section of the basement that had been framed in and carpeted. As she recalled, there was a pool table, a television and an old couch inside.

But when Tess went through the door, she stopped and gasped. "Oh, no. Not again."

A pale yellow candle flickered dimly in the centre of a circle drawn in chalk on the floor.

Tess turned to go back up the stairs but Arden stopped her. "Tess, it's not what you think. I needed to cast a circle for safety. The yellow candle is for peace and tranquillity."

Arden pulled Tess towards the circle. "Please sit here, facing south."

Tess yanked her arm away. "I'm not here to be a part of your voodoo ceremonies. I'm here to stop it. I want my dress back."

Arden skittered back, surprised. "Of course, Tess. It's over there." She gestured to an area near the pool table.

Tess squinted in the dim light. The dress was draped neatly over the back of a chair. No damage had been done to it but Tess couldn't be certain.

"Why did you want my dress?" Tess demanded. "So you could put some kind of hex on me?"

Arden folded her arms across her frail body. "No. I wanted to find you. I thought if I held an article of your clothing, I might be able to see were you were."

Tess turned her head, suspicously. "Did it work?"

Arden's shoulders slumped and she stared at the floor. "Of course not. I don't have any special power. I just thought I did."

"Then what's with the candle?" Tess gestured to the yellow candle flickering in the centre of the room.

"I said *I* didn't have any power." Arden took a step closer to Tess, glancing nervously towards the darkened corners of the basement. "But others do. We need to protect ourselves in whatever way we can by creating a safe space."

Tess picked up on Arden's fear and eyed a few of the corners of the room nervously. "Is there really such a thing?" she whispered.

Arden nodded. "There can be, if you think good strong thoughts." Arden took Tess's hand, pulling her back into the candlelight. "Now please, Tess – sit. And visualize all of the places that have made you feel safe and secure."

Tess did as she was told, simply because that was the one thing she really needed at the moment, to feel safe. She sat cross-legged in the circle, facing south. Arden sat beside her, then raised a metal cup from the floor by her knee. She held it out to Tess.

"This is milk, sugar and saffron," Arden explained. "You need to project that safe feeling into the milk. Then raise the cup with both hands and drink it."

Tess watched Arden drink first, waiting to see if the milk were somehow poisoned or drugged. But Arden seemed fine. She passed the cup to Tess, who drank, thinking the whole time of her snug attic bedroom, and of her mother and father and sister Kelly at home.

When the ceremony was completed, Tess asked, "Arden, do you have any idea what has been happening?"

Arden nodded. "Yes. And it's all my fault." She put her face in her hands. "I wish I'd never met Anthony Stokes. Or Meg or Carly. I wish my family had never moved here. I wish I could start over."

"Is that how this began?" Tess asked. "With Anthony?"

Arden nodded miserably and moved to a low table by the couch. A cigar box and a diary lay upon it. "After the fire last night, I couldn't face anyone. Meg was taken to the hospital with third degree burns on her legs and I don't know what happened to Carly. I ran home and hid down here. I've spent the night trying to sort out what went wrong, starting from the day I met Anthony and that despicable Ian."

"What a terrible person to have for a brother!"

"Oh, Ian's not his brother," Arden replied. "I'm not sure *what* he is, but I know they're not related. Ian worked for Anthony."

"That explains how surly he was," Tess murmured. "And his indifferent response to Anthony's death."

Arden flipped open the lid to the cigar box and lifted out a five-pointed star. It hung on a delicate silver chain. "Anthony gave this to me the day I lost the election for Student Council. He said I didn't need to be in that club, we'd form our own."

"We? Were Meg and Carly already involved with him?"

Arden nodded. "They followed him round like puppies. Meg was thrilled that such a handsome boy would even speak to her and Carly – she liked being with him because he was so different."

"Did he ask if you wanted to become a witch?"

Arden shook her head. "No, Anthony never used that term. Only the kids at school called us that. He asked me only if I believed in magic. And once we became a club, he called us his friends."

"So what did your club do?" Tess asked.

"Mostly we'd just hang out. And Anthony would demonstrate candle power. Each time we met, we'd have a ceremony and talk about who we liked or didn't like at school. During the ceremony we would fantasize ways of getting revenge. Anthony loved to hear that." Arden shifted uncomfortably in her seat. "Then one day one of our little fantasies actually came true. We couldn't wait to meet again to discuss it. That meeting Anthony brought an athame with him – that's a tiny dagger with magical words engraved on the handle. He told us it was a family heirloom. We used it in our ceremony, and before we knew it, we had dolls and powders and potions, and we were putting hexes on people."

Tess shook her head in dismay. "How could you, Arden?"

"Because I'd been hurt." Arden's face was set in hard lines of anger. "I lost the election and kids started shunning me in the halls, like they did when Ryan and I broke up. One minute I was going steady with Ryan, and the next, you'd taken him. I was with him first and you broke us up. Then *you* turned on *me*. Why?"

The audible pain in Arden's voice made Tess feel very guilty. It was true, Ryan had been with Arden when he and Tess first started dating. It had been an awkward situation and one Tess never really faced. "I guess I thought you'd be angry with me, so instead of just taking the heat, I got angry first and shut you out."

Arden stared at the pentacle in her hand.

"Well, whatever it was, Anthony met me when I was really down. And I have to admit it, I had fun getting revenge." She sighed heavily. "But then things turned sour."

"The book?" Tess said.

Arden nodded. "I never really questioned Anthony. I mean, all I knew was that he was this incredibly handsome boy from some exotic place. I didn't know what he was. Not even when I stole his book."

"What he was?" Tess repeated. "What do you mean? What was he?"

For this answer, Arden opened her diary. The latest entry was a numbered list. "I've been writing all night. I want people to know the truth – in case something happens to me."

Tess inhaled sharply and crossed to the couch to sit by Arden. Arden was frightened. As frightened as she was.

Tess read the first three items on the list out loud. "Cannot be seen in mirrors. Cannot be photographed. Cannot cross running water." She cocked her head and frowned. "This looks like a list of rules. But for who?"

Arden didn't reply but only gestured to the diary. "Read on."

"Can transform their bodies into other shapes. Like bats, wolves and—" Tess looked at Arden. "Cats."

Arden met Tess's gaze evenly. "For hundreds of years this part of Massachussets has been home to supernatural events. In 1692 nineteen women were burned as witches in Salem. Secret covens have been meeting ever since. I supposed it would make sense that...other spirits would walk this earth, too."

Tess's throat had gone dry. She had to swallow several times before she could even speak. "What are you talking about, Arden?"

"Anthony wasn't—" Arden pursed her lips. "Human."

The hair on the back of Tess's neck tingled. Her heart pounded, her palms felt moist. "Why do you think that?" she whispered.

"The list." Arden pointed to the diary. "Anthony refused to have his photograph taken for the yearbook. Or at the homecoming dance. Once Meg brought a camera to our circle and he got so angry, he smashed it. And the reflection—"

"He didn't have one," Tess gasped, wide-eyed. "I remember now. I received a note at the party, asking me to meet him in the library. I thought it might be from Anthony, so I went. I was facing the fireplace. I heard movement behind me. When I looked into the mirror, I saw only my face. Yet when I turned round he was standing directly behind me."

Arden nodded slowly. "He refused to cross the foot bridge over Tolman Creek, he always insisted on taking the long way round. During the day, he was pale and subdued. It wasn't until nightfall, after the sun had set, that he really came alive."

Tess moved instinctively from the couch back to the candle, closer to the circle of safety. "So what you're telling me is—"

Arden joined her in the circle and clutched Tess's hand in hers.

"Anthony was a vampire."

CHAPTER ELEVEN

Ding-dong.

"Don't answer it," Tess rasped to Arden. "Please."

Arden put one finger to her lips and whispered, "My mom is home. She'll probably get it."

Tess didn't know how long they had huddled in the circle of safety, holding hands. Long enough for Arden's mother to return and the candle to nearly burn out. She was certain night had fallen outside.

Footsteps sounded across the floor above their heads. They heard the front door creak open. They held their breaths.

"Trick or treat, trick or treat, give us something good to eat!" a chorus of little voices shouted.

Arden exhaled loudly in relief. "Oh, god, I

forgot," she said, with a chuckle. "It's Halloween."

"Kids are going to be ringing your doorbell all night," Tess said.

Arden stepped across the room to get her box. Inside were several crude homemade crosses that she'd made by tying together sticks with string. She handed one to Tess and kept one for herself. "Kids in masks and costumes. We won't be able to tell the good guys from the bad guys."

Tess clutched her cross to her chest, suddenly chilled. "Arden," she whispered, "who are the bad guys?"

Arden went to her bookshelf and took down a book titled *The Silver Spiral*. "I told you – Ian, for one. He was Anthony's servant, but now that Anthony's gone, I think Ian wants his power."

"Does that mean Ian is a...a..."

Arden shook her head. "I don't think so. I went through my books trying to find everything I could about vampires. They seem to need people to help them. So they find weak souls like Ian to do their bidding."

Tess thought of Carly, snarling and hissing

like a cat as she lunged at Ian. "Is Carly one of those souls, too?"

Arden shut her eyes. "I think so. But I don't think she was working for Anthony. I think she belongs to someone else."

"There's someone else?" Tess knew the answer before the words were out of her mouth. "That dark figure. In the corner."

Arden's hands were now shaking so badly, she couldn't hold her book. It fell on the floor by her feet. "Oh, god!" she moaned. "Why did we steal that book? Anthony was right, we were amateurs. We should never have taken it."

"Are you saying *you* called up that – that shadow?"

Arden nodded. "We had cast our circle and lit our candles. Our plan was to put a hex on everyone that we hated at the party." She dropped her head. "You were one of them."

"But the shadow—"

"We opened the grimoire, Anthony's *Book of Shadows*, and chose a spell that harnessed the powers of darkness."

"What?"

Arden shook her head. "We were silly. It

147

sounded so dramatic and strange. Carly especially liked the idea of having power over all of you." Arden's fingers held the cross so tightly, Tess could see her knuckles turn white. "But when we began the incantation, something shifted. We didn't harness any power. We seemed to give it all away. I felt drained and dizzy. The next thing I knew the window had flown open and something flapped into the room."

"Bat!" Tess cried. "It was a bat."

Arden blinked at Tess. "I believe it was."

"That's what Ryan was trying to tell me," Tess said excitedly. "Anthony had brought him to his knees with one hand but what made Anthony release Ryan wasn't me or Ian. It was the bat!"

Arden knelt down and picked up her book. Her hands trembled violently as she flipped through the pages. "I think we need to cast another circle, Tess. I'm feeling very frightened just talking about this." She found the page she was looking for and then took a small box of votive candles from a shelf. "We need to surround ourselves with love and good will. I'll pick a candle that represents each of us. What's your sign?"

"Taurus," Tess said. She was starting to feel a little dizzy, from lack of sleep and food.

"Your candle would be green. I'm a Pisces so mine would be blue."

The image of the bat flying into the room formed in Tess's mind. Then that of the dark figure in the corner. And the room began to spin...

He was there. The room filled with choking, acrid smoke and her legs locked. He helped her, gently pushing her towards Meg, whose dress was on fire. As Tess moved, something struck her foot. She stopped, reached down, felt the smooth leather cover of the *Book of Shadows*.

"Not so fast!"

Tess was yanked back, although the other girls escaped. Tess heard them screaming, "Fire! Everybody, run!" as they fled out of the room.

Anthony hurled her across the room. She fell in a corner, surrounded by flames and choking smoke.

She lay stunned, unable to move. Pain

pulsed in her head from hitting something sharp, but still she held the book in her arms.

Through the smoke, Anthony commanded, "Give me the book, Tess. Now."

Tess could barely breathe. Unseen hands lifted her to her feet. A voice – how did she know it was the shadow in the corner's voice? – whispered in her ear. "Hold tight to the book," he said. "It is your shield and will protect you."

Anthony came towards her, huge and menacing, the whites of his eyes glowing red as coals.

Tess had never been so frightened in her life. The fire was about to cut off her last possible route of escape. The heat was so intense her skin felt as if it was boiling.

"Master!" Ian's voice, raw with panic, cut through the smoke. "Master! He's here!"

Anthony turned his head for a fraction of a second. And—

"Here, drink this."

Arden held a glass of orange juice to Tess's lips. With a start Tess realized she had slumped to the floor.

"You passed out," Arden explained, dabbing at Tess's forehead with a cool, damp face flannel.

Tess drank the entire glass of juice in one gulp. "I haven't eaten all day," she explained. "And I think I'm a little dizzy from lack of sleep."

"I'll make you a sandwich," Arden said, getting to her feet. "You're going to need to be strong. To face what lies ahead."

"No, no," Tess whimpered softly, catching Arden's hand. "Anthony's gone. The book is lost. Couldn't it just be over?"

"I'm afraid it's only just begun," Arden said in a weary voice. "Through our stupidity, Meg, Carly and I brought something unspeakably evil to Brookston."

"But you had nothing to do with Anthony coming here," Tess said. "He moved here on his own."

"But we stole Anthony's grimoire and used it to call his worst enemy – someone far more powerful and deadly than Anthony could ever have been."

"The shape in the corner," Tess murmured. "He spoke to me." She unconsciously raised her hand to her left ear. "Whispered in my ear."

Arden's eyes grew wide. "Did he touch you?"

Tess pursed her lips. "Yes. I think so. He helped me up, after Anthony threw me against the wall. Why?"

Arden hurried to get her diary. "There are rules that govern all forces. But he only touched you once, right?" She flipped through her diary till she reached the page with the rules. "Three bites from a vampire and you are his."

"Three bites?" Tess pressed the flannel to her face. "You can't be serious. This is like something made up. A movie!"

"Tess, for us to protect ourselves and draw strength from our personal power, we need to believe in the impossible. You've seen its effects. You more than others should believe."

Tess took a deep breath. "OK, say that Carly is under a spell cast by this strange figure. Why would she try to help me? When Ian was trying to find the book, Carly protected us."

"That would make sense," Arden said, "because her controlling spirit wants the grimoire for himself."

"So the book of spells – this *Book of Shadows* – it's that powerful?" asked Tess.

Arden nodded. "The shadow figure knows that the spell which summoned him here in the first place can also banish him for ever. That's why he's so desperate to get that book."

"You mean if we find the *Book of Shadows* first," Tess said, "we can put an end to this evil?"

"I suppose so." Arden looked dubious. "Although you saw what happened the last time we amateurs tried something."

"So you don't have it?" demanded Tess.

"The book?" Arden looked at her quizzically. "No. I lost it during the fire."

Tess stopped walking. "I was never a part of your group. The only magic I know is a few stupid card tricks." Her frustration boiled out of her. "So why does everyone think *I* know where this *Book of Shadows* is?"

Arden stared at Tess and said simply, "Because you took it from the party."

Tess was on the roof of the mansion's porch. Below, party guests were pouring out of the front doors in a mad torrent of pushing, shoving bodies, trampling the slow or injured.

In the distance she heard the sound of wailing sirens as the fire trucks approached. Looking over the edge of the porch Tess saw there was a car below her. She leapt on to the roof of the car and slid down the windshield. It was a struggle to get off the hood of the car because her hands gripped a very large leather book.

"I *did* have it." Tess cocked her head and looked at Arden. "I did leave the party with the book. I remember now."

"Good." Arden smiled for the first time since Tess had arrived. "Where did you go then?"

Tess tried to think. "I know I wound up in an alley off the town square," she said. "But how I got there...I can't remember!"

"Tess, you must!" insisted Arden.

Tess shut her eyes tightly, determined to recall everything.

She was on the ground, stumbling forward. People were running into Tess, fighting to get away from the inferno. Her ears rang with the screams of the injured, and of those still trapped inside the burning Hawthorne Mansion.

She heard people call her name. She recognized Ryan's voice, and Rose's. But she was too dazed to find them.

She wandered blindly, not aware that she'd lost one of her shoes.

Tess stumbled on to the road leading from the mansion back to the town centre.

From the opposite direction, dozens of emergency vehicles – fire trucks, police cars, ambulances – screamed by her, heading for the fire. Dazed, she barely reached the shoulder of the road before one of them nearly ran her over.

She'd lost everything – everything but the book. She clutched it to her chest, like a child hugging a teddy bear. Knowing she possessed the book was all that kept her going.

Finally, blocks from the mansion, the fire further and further from her senses, she snapped out of her shock.

She looked round, noticing where her wandering had brought her.

"Of course I would come here," she murmured to herself. "Of course."

She looked down at the leather book. It had survived the fire intact. Just like Tess.

Knowing its importance, sensing its power, she found a place to bury it. Deep under the stony New England soil. Deep, where no one but she would know where to look.

"Tess? Tess!" Arden shook her by the shoulders. "Tess, do you remember?"

"Come on." Tess jumped to her feet and headed for the basement stairs. "I know where the book is. Let's just hope we're not too late!"

CHAPTER TWELVE

Your Moon in Aries makes you one forceful,
independent little bull. But be careful, its
placement in the sixth house also makes your
health uncertain. You could be susceptible to
drugs or drink, or even poisoned apples.
Keep your eyes wide open.

On a normal Halloween it was a lark to run
up and down the block, seeing how many
houses you could visit before it became too
cold or late to continue. In years past it was fun
to walk up to homes with flashing strobe
lights, fake cobwebs, and scary sounds coming
from hidden speakers.

But not this year. Every time a ghost or
werewolf passed them, the girls worried for a
moment that it might be the real thing.

Holding hands, Tess and Arden made their

way past scores of witches, devils, vampires, monsters, mummies, cats, and zombies. It was as if the evil already had taken over Brookston.

"Slow down," Arden huffed as they raced downtown. "I can't keep up."

"Come on!" Tess tugged at Arden's hand. "If I figured it out, someone else might, too!"

Arden nodded and smiled. A smile of genuine friendship.

Funny how things turn out, Tess thought. *Here's Arden, about the last person I would've counted on in a crisis, running to help me.*

They reached the town green. Across it, Tess could see the dinner crowd just leaving the Pewter Platter.

The girls hurried on.

A few moments later, Tess looked up. "There it is," she said.

The First Church of Brookston.

In her shock and delirium after the fire on Friday night, Tess had somehow had the sense to wander there.

And – though she wasn't absolutely positive – she had a good idea exactly where she had buried the leather book of spells.

She led Arden to the church's front steps, and gestured towards the minister's favourite flowerbed. The one with freshly turned soil and dominated by the white wooden cross in the centre.

A place no vampire would dare breach.

Arden nodded her head. "Brilliant!"

Tess sank her fingernails into the dirt, frozen after another cold night. At first the rocky ground refused to give way, so Tess got to her feet and kicked it repeatedly with the heel of her shoe. The blows caused the top layer to separate, enough at least that she could continue to dig in with her fingertips.

Arden worked beside her. The two soon removed the top layer. The dirt underneath was more densely packed. Still, they dug until their fingers and hands ached.

With the pile of rubble growing higher, Tess finally felt something hard resist her fingers.

"I've got it!" she said.

She and Arden concentrated their digging on the spot. Slowly the book came into view.

"Grab it," Arden said. "Now let's get out of here."

"No," Tess rasped. "We should stay here at

the church. We'll be safe here."

Arden shivered in the evening chill. "I hope you're right."

Just holding the book, Tess could sense its power. Her palms quivered from the waves of energy vibrating off the pages. She solemnly passed it to Arden. "Here is the book, Arden. Do you think you can use it to somehow reverse the evil you brought here, and make that spirit disappear?"

Arden stared at the book, not even daring to touch it. "Oh, Tess!" Arden whimpered. "I'm so frightened. I don't know if I can pull this off."

"Look." Tess tried to make her voice sound commanding, when her insides were really quivering mush. "You brought him to Brookston. You must make him disappear. I think you need to revisit the ceremony you performed."

Arden swallowed and accepted the book.

"Only this time," Tess continued, "end it differently."

"What if the figure shows up and stops us?" Arden asked, concerned.

"We'll arm ourselves with crosses and

garlic and all the other things that vampires can't stand," Tess said.

"I don't like this," Arden said, still holding the book in front of her, not daring to open the cover.

Tess touched her shoulder. "Arden, you told me we have to believe in our own goodness. That will protect us."

Arden had a very worried look on her face. "Tess, I'm not as strong as you are. I thought I was, but after the fire and..."

Things weren't turning out as Tess had hoped. It was Arden who was supposed to lead her through the casting of the spells – and now the tables had been turned. Tess was going to have to make the decisions. "OK, here's the deal. We make a circle of safety. You find the spell that harnessed the powers of darkness. You tell me what items we need to cast to spell – and I'll get them."

"You'll get them?" Arden repeated. "But you can't leave me here alone."

Tess scooped up a handful of dirt and heaved it at the side of the church's foundation. "I won't leave you. I'll call someone. My sister. Kelly will help."

"Kelly? But she's only eleven."

"We live right across the park. She can be here in five minutes. If I ask her to get the materials she'll do it. Believe me."

Arden chewed her lip, trying to think fast. "All right," she said finally. "I'll do it. I hope we make it through this night."

Tess hugged Arden and then stood up. While Arden carefully turned the pages of the grimoire, Tess paced anxiously.

She thought about her family, hoping she would see them again.

She thought about Ryan, wondering if her first serious relationship was over for good.

She thought about Sebastian. He had become such an important part of her life so quickly. She hoped he'd be waiting for her on Monday, when this horrible episode was over.

"OK," Arden announced, holding up a small piece of paper that she'd pulled from her pocket. It was lucky she'd brought along a pen, though she had trouble getting it to write at first because of the cold night air. "I've made my list. Let's call Kelly."

Tess was reluctant to leave the church grounds, but the nearest pay phone was across the street on the corner of the town square. "Leave the book here," Tess instructed. "Under that cross – and bring your list."

After making an elaborate check of all the darkened areas surrounding the pay phone, the girls opened the booth and squeezed inside. Tess put in her quarter and dialled. Kelly answered it on one ring. "Langleys'. Hello?"

"It's me," Tess said, not even daring to say her name for fear someone on the street might hear. "Now listen, Kell, I need your help."

Kelly covered the mouthpiece and called, "Sorry, Mom, it's just Jennifer. She wants to know when I'm going out trick-or-treating. I know. I'm telling her I'm not going."

"Wait!" Tess shouted. "Tell Mom you *are* going. For just a little while."

"Oh, wait, change that," Kelly called. "I need to go out for just a little while. Because—" She paused, trying to think of a convenient fib.

"Because I want some chocolate and you know me, I hate to spend my allowance," Tess prompted.

Kelly repeated her words exactly, then whispered back into the receiver, "Very funny."

"Now listen, Kell, do you have a piece of paper? I need you to gather some things from the house and bring them to the church as soon as you can."

Kelly's voice was muffled and Tess could tell she had ducked her head into the broom cupboard to talk. "The church? Is that where you are? Reverend Mooney has been calling here, scared about what may be taking place in our community."

"He said that to Mom and Dad?"

"In so many words. He didn't offer any explanations except he kept muttering, 'These are dangerous times.'"

"How do you know, did he come over?"

"No, I listened in on the extension. The Reverend didn't feel comfortable leaving his church. He said he felt he needed to be there to help."

Tess looked back at the church. The windows were dark. "Well, if he was there earlier, he's not any more."

"Hmm," Kelly murmured. "That's strange."

"Now listen, get a pen and write this down."

"Got it," Kelly replied.

"We need a green, blue, or yellow candle.

And definitely a black one."

"We only have white ones," Kelly whispered.

"She only has white ones," Tess told Arden.

"Just bring what she has," Arden said.

"I heard," Kelly said. "OK. What else?"

Tess handed the phone to Arden, who read, "A cup of milk mixed with sugar. Some salt in water."

"No problem."

"Now we get to the hard things," Arden said. "A circle of blue cloth."

"I'll look through Mom's sewing closet," Kelly whispered. "You can't believe the stuff she keeps in there."

"A silver crescent moon," Arden said.

Tess grabbed the phone. "I have those crescent earrings in my jewellery box. Bring one and a string of white thread."

Arden continued to read from her list of herbs and spices, making substitutions where she had to. Then she handed the phone back to Tess.

"Did you get all that, Kelly?" Tess asked.

"Yes," Kelly replied. "But who was that?"

"Arden," Tess whispered. "She's helping me."

"Arden!" Kelly bellowed in full voice. "Are you out of your mind? Tess, she's a witch! She's not going to help you. She's going to hurt you. Get away from her now!"

"Kelly, she's OK – believe me! Now don't argue and do what I tell you," Tess commanded. "This is a matter of life and death. As soon as you get what I've asked for, bring it to me. I'll be waiting behind the church."

"Kelly, what are you shouting about?" Tess heard her mother call in the background.

"Nothing, Mom," Kelly said as she moved to hang up the phone. "It's Jennifer's costume. She needs a few things to finish it and I have to get them to her before Halloween's over and the neighbours run out of candy."

Tess smiled as she heard the click and the dial tone. She turned to Arden. "She's on her way."

True to her word, Kelly arrived in less than fifteen minutes. Dressed in a clown costume, complete with red nose and trick-or-treat bag, Kelly pedalled her bike to the side of the church, then raced round the back to find Tess.

"Here's the stuff. I had a hard time finding

everything." She thrust her trick-or-treat bag in Tess's hands, then bent over and put her hands on her knees, gasping for breath. "Mom made me wear my costume, or I would have been here sooner."

Tess handed Arden the bag and hugged Kelly. "Good work, sis. I knew you'd come through."

Kelly watched as Arden moved beneath the back safety light of the church and quickly examined the bag's contents. Kelly tugged on her sister's arm. "I brought what you asked for," she said. "Now will you tell me what you're planning to do?"

In as few words as possible, Tess relayed the events of the day. As Kelly listened, her jaw dropped open. Every few seconds she'd gasp, "That's incredible!" or, "I don't believe it!" as Tess told her about the discovery of the book and what had really happened at the Hawthorne Mansion.

"So you think this guy, this evil person, killed Anthony and set the mansion on fire?" Kelly asked.

"I think the fire was accidental," Tess replied. "But I'm certain he murdered

Anthony. Arden knows, she can tell you."

Arden, who was carefully filling her small fabric pouch with the herbs Kelly had brought them, shook her head. "I don't know. I wasn't in the room."

"But if that strange spirit didn't kill Anthony, who did?" Tess asked, mystified.

Arden carefully tied the bag of herbs on to the white string and looped it round Tess's neck. "When I escaped from that room there were only three people left inside."

Rose's description of the fire suddenly popped into Tess's mind as she said slowly, "Anthony, the mysterious figure and me."

Arden nodded. "So you must have witnessed the murder."

Tess closed her eyes and she was back in the room...

Trapped! Anthony stepped forward through the smoke and loomed ominously above her. "Give me the book, Tess. Now."

Tess could barely breathe.

"The book!" Anthony shouted.

Weeping, choking, Tess held on to the book with all her might.

168

She'd never been so frightened in her life. She could see the fire was about to cut off her only escape. The heat was so intense that her skin felt as if it was boiling.

"Master!" Ian's voice cut through the smoke. "Master! Behind you!"

Anthony turned his head for a fraction of a second...

And now Tess remembered something new. She remembered looking down and being stunned to find that a wooden candle holder had been thrust into her hands. A long, thin wooden spike protruded from one end.

Anthony spun back round. He was unrecognizable now. His eyes were black ovals of seething malice; his teeth like a fierce animal's, with foam bubbling at the corners of his mouth. He sprang at her.

Without thinking, Tess thrust the candle spike at his heart.

His flesh hissed as something pushed on her arm, hard. The spike was driven deeper and deeper into his body.

"Oh my god!" In horror Tess let go of the spike, which was now buried deep in Anthony's chest.

The vampire's face registered successive waves of agony and hatred as he staggered from the mortal wound. In shocked surprise, he looked over Tess's shoulder and gasped, "You!"

Tess wanted to turn and look, but the mysterious stranger who had saved her from the flames wrapped his arms round her, folding her into his darkness. He pulled her close. Something warm pierced her neck, sending her pulse fluttering as fast as a hummingbird's wings. Tess had never known such bliss. She closed her eyes, relishing the moment – and then he was gone. And she was standing alone on the roof...

"Oh my god!" Tess slowly brought her hands to her face. "The murderer was me!"

CHAPTER THIRTEEN

Shock. Fear. Resolve. Those were the emotions felt by Arden, Kelly and Tess.

Shock that Tess could do such a heinous thing. "My own sister a murderer!" Kelly had gasped.

Fear of the repercussions. "You can't just drive a stake through a person's heart and get away with it," Arden had warned.

And a fierce resolve to plunge forward. Now they knew for certain that something foul and evil had come to their town. Somehow Tess had been able to stop Anthony. If she could eliminate him, why not his enemy?

"A stake," Tess cried. "We need a wooden stake."

Tess hurried over to Reverend Mooney's garden and started prising loose one of the pickets from the fence bordering it. She remembered seeing the minister sprinkle holy water over his garden, consecrating the soil. Hopefully that would make the stake more powerful.

"I'm so scared!" Kelly cried.

"Don't be," Tess ordered. "If we're afraid, we're dead."

She wiped the dirt from one of the stakes on her jeans, then hid it inside her jacket.

"Let's go," she said.

"I thought we were doing the ceremony here," Arden said.

"I don't think he'll come near the church," Tess said.

"But why do we need to call him?" Kelly was trying to act brave, but Tess could see her knees were trembling. "I mean, isn't the idea to send him away?"

Arden put one hand on Kelly's shoulder. "We need to call him so we can cast a spell binding his evil and send him back to wherever he came from." Arden faced Tess. "Where should we do it?"

Tess pointed up the hill behind the church. "The crest of the hill. It's just beyond the cemetery."

Arden nodded. "And on unconsecrated ground."

The girls were about to climb over the low cemetery wall when they heard someone shout, "Tess! Wait!"

Ryan?

Tess glanced at Arden, but had no time to say a word before he ran up.

Ryan tried to hug Tess, but she pulled away.

"How did you know I'd be here?" she asked, suspiciously.

"I called him," Kelly confessed, ducking her head to whisper to Tess. "When you said you were with, um, Arden, I was afraid for you."

"Look, I just want to help," Ryan said. "I'll do whatever you need."

Tess smiled. *Maybe he isn't so bad after all.*

Arden, who was standing nearby holding the book, called, "Ryan can't be with us, Tess. Not in our circle."

Tess nodded. "In order for this to work, you'll need to stay out of sight," she told Ryan. "Stay by the church."

"Whatever you say," Ryan agreed. He took her hand and squeezed it tightly. "I hope you know what you're doing."

Tess took a shaky breath. "So do I."

Without warning, the air was split by a flash of lightning that struck a nearby tree, sending a heavy limb crashing to the ground. And then a sound, barely perceptible to the others, was heard by Tess. It was the rumble of an engine, idling. *The black car.*

"He's here," Tess rasped. "We'd better get started."

Ryan hid behind the church as the girls stepped over the low stone wall and headed up the hillside.

Tess had never been in the cemetery at night, and it was creepy. Shadows played deceptive tricks on the gravestones. Strange sounds came from the creaking old trees. The wind whipped dead leaves round in miniature cyclones.

They reached the top of the hill just beyond the cemetery wall, near the tree where Tess had first glimpsed the smoldering ruins of the Hawthorne Mansion. Where she had met Sebastian for the first time.

Will I ever see him again?

She pushed the thought out of her mind and

got to work.

Arden opened the *Book of Shadows*. "I need the blue cloth," she told Tess. "Kelly, did you bring that earring?"

Tess laid the blue cloth in a circle. To it, Kelly added the silver crescent moon earring.

The girls formed a ring and held hands. They sat down as one. Arden took a white candle from the bag and lit it. Tess held a cup of milk mixed with sugar with both hands.

"Now look at the candle flame and visualize three women," Arden instructed. "One dressed in white, another in red, a third in black. Let them move together and merge into one woman. Imagine her placing her hands over us and saying, 'Children, I am with you.'"

The clouds began to swirl madly above their heads yet the air round them remained perfectly still.

"Blessed be, between the worlds, in all the worlds, protect us tonight," Arden chanted. "So mote it be."

Then she turned to another page of the book and said, "We're ready to call forth the mysterious stranger."

While Arden lit the candle she instructed

Tess to sprinkle a bottle of salt water on the ground. Then she chanted again.

"Blessed be, by art changed, by art unmade. We cast a silver net to fall over you. By air and earth, by water and fire, so be you bound. Come to us, o powerful evil. Come, so we may destroy you."

A warm, sweet wind gushed up the hill. It was so strong that it blew the candle out and nearly knocked the girls over. The earth shook. Lightning rained from the dark sky and a dense fog flowed up the hill and round the tiny circle of friends.

"I can't hold on!" Arden cried as the *Book of Shadows* slipped out of her hands and began to rise into the air. Tess lunged forward and jerked it back. She clutched it to her chest, using every ounce of strength she had.

"Tess, I'm so afraid!" Kelly whimpered, pressing herself against her sister.

But Tess was no longer seated on the ground. She felt herself being lifted in the air.

"Run!" she screamed to Kelly and Arden. "Run to the church. And don't look back."

The fog grew thicker and thicker. Tess could just make out the shapes of her sister and

Arden, running away down the hill.

"Run, Kelly," she whispered. "With all your might."

Slowly the fog spun her in a great descending gyre, a silver spiral of mist. Then the spinning stopped and she was lowered gently to the ground. The fog dissipated into tiny puffs of clouds floating along the ground.

"Hello, Tess."

Stunned, Tess took a moment to orient herself. She was still by the cemetery. She was still holding the leather-bound book of spells, the *Book of Shadows*.

She looked up. The mysterious figure, his face shrouded in shadow, stood under the naked limbs of the ash trees, just outside the cemetery wall.

"What do you want from me?" she asked, her voice shaking with fear.

"I don't want to hurt you," he said. "There's no reason to hurt you. Anthony and Ian – they opposed me. So they had to die." His voice was warm and resonant, almost thrilling to hear. He seemed to caress the air with his words. "But you, Tess, you have the chance to live for ever."

"Live forever?" she repeated.

"From the moment I saw you at the party, I knew you were unique," the figure explained. "Beautiful, yes. But I've known many beautiful women in my long life. You possess something else."

"I don't understand," she said. She glanced down at her hands. They still held fast to the book, yet trembled violently as successive waves of panic convulsed her body.

"Come to me, Tess," he said, his voice haunting, coaxing. "Come. Let me complete the ritual that shall make you mine for ever. Together we can rule the night."

"No," Tess announced, defiantly.

Suddenly, the figure became impatient. "I have no time to argue with you, child. Bring me the book."

"And if I don't?" Tess asked.

"I shall destroy everything that matters to you," he said coldly. "Your family. Your friends. Your town. And I shall make you watch before damning you to a never-ending torment!"

Tess felt her knees growing weak. "Please," she murmured. "You don't want me."

"But I do," the figure replied. "See how strong, how ingenious you've been in piecing together what happened at the party." There was a rustle, like wings, and the figure stepped towards her. "I've travelled so far, across an ocean of eternity, to find you. Now I really can't let you go."

He raised his hand and Tess found herself gently floating over the ground.

He opened his arms and she floated against him. Tess shut her eyes, trying to will her limbs to resist but it was useless. He folded her in his arms and pressed her body close.

"Twice I have left my mark," he whispered. "Now, with the third one, you shall be mine for all time."

Twice? Tess thought. Once at the party. But the second time?

And then she figured it out.

"Oh, god!" she screamed, struggling to free herself. "Let me go!"

He held her tightly. He turned his head and lowered his mouth towards her neck.

"No! No!" Tess screamed.

She felt his lips part. Warm, sticky air rushed against her flesh.

Suddenly someone, a boy, leapt on the figure's back. Tess managed to pull free as the vampire and the boy fell to the ground. She scrambled over to the cemetery wall, huddling against the cold stones.

In the darkness it was difficult to see who the boy was. He took the vampire's head and rammed it against the cold ground. He was about to do it again, but the vampire threw him off and pounced on him.

Tess saw the gleam of the demon's teeth an instant before they plunged into the boy's neck.

The boy let out an agonized scream of pain. Somehow, blood spurting from his neck, he managed to wriggle away and get to his feet. His features were clearly visible in the moonlight.

"Ryan!" Tess shouted. "Ryan, no! He'll kill you!"

But Ryan lowered his head and rammed into the vampire, knocking him backwards on to the ground. Ryan looked round, then picked up a rock, determined to smash the vampire's skull. But with incredible speed the vampire leapt up and was at Ryan before he could react.

"Stop it!" Tess shrieked.

The vampire then knocked Ryan down with a blow between the shoulders. Falling on Ryan's back, it delivered another deep, bloody bite.

Tess couldn't stand by and watch another second. She had to do something.

"You can have the book," she cried. "Here it is." Tess threw it at him, then dropped to her knees, sobbing. "Here I am."

The vampire rose to his full height. He scooped up the book, then turned back towards Ryan, who lay writhing on the ground. Blood flowed from the twin wounds on his neck.

For a moment Tess was afraid the vampire was going to finish him off. Instead, he helped Ryan to his feet. And then he did the strangest thing – he embraced Ryan, as if they were long lost brothers.

Once the figure let go of him, Ryan sank to the ground. His body lay twisted, covered with dirt and bits of dried grass and leaves.

The dark figure dusted himself off. "No more surprises?" he asked.

Tess smiled but didn't rise.

A fragrant breeze began to ruffle her hair.

As the figure approached her, Tess could feel her body aching to feel his touch. To fold herself into his open arms.

Tess fought against the feeling and as he lifted her gently to her feet, she whispered, "I do have one last surprise."

"And what is that, my love?" he murmured, bending his head towards her neck.

"This."

Tess ripped the wooden stake from beneath her jacket and plunged it into his chest with all her might. Surprisingly it penetrated his skin like a knife going through warm butter. He fell back against the cemetery wall, clutching at it with both hands.

"No," he moaned, as a hideous black liquid gurgled from his mouth. He held out his hands, pleading, imploring her to help him. "Please."

"Damn you to hell," she said, and shoved him over the wall into the cemetery.

He staggered to his feet, then fell forward, tumbling down the hill toward the church below.

Tess rushed to Ryan.

He was still alive, but losing blood quickly. She dashed down the hill, following the path the vampire's body had blazed. Literally, as the earth was scorched where he had rolled over it.

Near the church Tess found Arden and Kelly standing over the vampire's body, where it had come to rest against a tombstone.

"Is he dead?" Tess asked.

Arden stared back dully, her face a blank mask of fear.

"Ryan's hurt," Tess told her. "Can you go and check on him?"

Arden nodded dumbly and stumbled up the hill.

Tess bent down and rolled the figure on to his back. The stake remained impaled in his heart. The book was still gripped in his left hand. There were no signs of life.

"A match," Tess murmured to Kelly as she pulled the book from his hands. "I need a match." Kelly fumbled in the bag she'd brought and produced a book of matches, then knelt beside Tess.

Tess struck the match and set fire to the open book. The ancient pages, fluttering like dry leaves in the breeze, exploded into flame. In the few seconds it took for the book to burn,

Tess took one last look at the vampire's face.

A wail of pain and horror filled the night air as Tess and Kelly watched the perfect, handsome face – Sebastian's beautiful face – shrivel and rot, then disintegrate into a fine white dust.

CHAPTER FOURTEEN

Transiting Neptune now eases out of tricky
Gemini to begin a lengthy sojourn in Cancer.
You'll feel much better and your disposition
will improve as Neptune sextiles your natal
sun. But stay down to earth, Taurus – don't
get too dreamy!

*I*n hindsight, it wasn't difficult seeing the
clues to Sebastian's real identity.

That first morning when Tess had met him,
he had claimed not to know the murder
victim's name but later said his name was
Anthony. She'd never told Sebastian her last
name yet he said he'd found her address in the
phone book. Sebastian appeared and
disappeared suddenly, always accompanied by
that black car or a creeping fog. He refused to
cross running water. All signs mentioned in

Arden's list.

Ryan was lucky. The wounds on his neck were superficial and when he came down the hill with Arden, he was only a little bit dizzy. Ryan had joined hands in the churchyard with Tess, Kelly and Arden, vowing never to talk about what they had witnessed that Halloween night. What was done was done. The nightmare was over.

And there was a second small miracle that Halloween. As the four of them said goodbye at the church, Carly stumbled out of the shadows, completely dazed.

"You're alive!" Tess shouted.

"What...what happened?" Carly mumbled, rubbing her eyes. "I feel like I've been asleep for days." When she looked up at them, it was clear she was herself again. The cat's eyes were gone.

Tess shot a silent look at Arden, then replied, "You were hurt at the Halloween party last night, but now you're OK. And so's Meg."

When Tess and Kelly arrived home, Kelly told their parents she'd found Tess when she was out trick-or-treating. Tess managed to convince them that the fiery tragedy had traumatized her so that she hadn't known what she was doing that Halloween. Mostly their mom and dad were grateful and relieved to have Tess back, safe and sound.

The police talked to Tess and accepted her version of Anthony's death – that in the rush to get out of the inferno, he had tripped and fallen on the candle holder. Lacking any hard evidence, Anthony's death and the fire were both ruled a terrible accident.

A month passed. Thanksgiving came and went, and now the town of Brookston was preparing for Christmas. The stores were loaded with merchandise and the streets were decorated with full holiday cheer.

One evening a few days before Christmas, dozens of people were braving the evening chill and soft snowfall to take in the sights. Among them were Tess and Ryan, walking hand in hand past the Pewter Platter.

"What's this movie you're dying to see?" she asked.

"You'll find out when we turn the corner," he replied.

She leant against him for warmth – but also because they'd been getting along fantastically since that horrible Halloween night.

At the corner they turned towards the Brookston Cinema. Tess read the titles illuminated on the overhead canopy. There was the usual holiday fare, and a romance.

"*Eternally Yours*," Ryan said, reading the title aloud. "I thought you'd like that."

Tess smiled at the change in him. A few months before, Ryan would never have dreamt of taking her to a movie like that.

"Hi," he said to the ticket seller. "Two for *Eternally Yours*."

Tess heard the click of the machine printing the tickets. She heard Ryan slide his money through the small slot.

"Are you sure you want to see this one?" she asked.

"Why not?" Ryan asked, scooping up his change. "You've always bugged me to take you to these kinds of movies – so now I am."

"Well, I think it's sweet, Ryan, but..."

"But what?"

"It's just not like you, to be the least bit gushy or romantic—"

"Hey!" he interrupted. "I've changed. I'm not the guy I used to be."

"I know but—"

"Trust me," Ryan said, taking her arm and leading her inside. "Have I ever steered you wrong?"

She was about to laugh – when they passed by the open glass doors.

In the glass, Tess caught a glimpse of her own reflection, dressed in winter coat with red beret perched on her thick dark hair. Her eyes grew wide with shock.

Shock, because the glass reflected not even a hint of Ryan, who was pulling her inside – inside towards the large, dark theatre.

*ZODIAC

*ARIES*TAURUS*GEMINI*CANCER*LEO*VIRGO*LIBRA*
*SCORPIO*SAGITTARIUS*CAPRICORN*AQUARIUS*PISCES*

Twelve signs of the Zodiac. Twelve novels, each one embracing the characteristics of a zodiac sign. Pushed to the extreme, these characteristics lead down twisting paths into tales of mystery, horror, romance and fantasy.

Whatever your sun sign, you will want to read Zodiac, the series written in the stars.

SERIES CREATED BY JAHNNA N. MALCOLM

CANCER:
EMOTIONAL, CARING
DARK SHADOWS

*C*hloe works tirelessly in her garden to create something beautiful, but nothing seems to flourish. Is it because a murderer used to live in the house before Chloe and her brother moved in? Then, a secret helper transforms the garden overnight – a secret helper who doesn't want Chloe to know his identity. Can the murder be linked to him and can caring Chloe put the pieces of the chain together?

LIBRA:
FAIR-MINDED, ROMANTIC
FROZEN IN TIME

*L*ily lives for her painting. With her boyfriend, she creates a mural that grows ever more beautiful as her own life becomes harsher. Then her boyfriend is killed by a gang. Has Lily lost him forever? If only she could be with him still in the beautiful world of the painting...

SCORPIO:
PASSIONATE, FORCEFUL
DEATH GRIP

*S*abrina loves with a fierce intensity - even those who have died. First her mother drowns, and then Matt... Can *his* death really have been an accident or was it cold-blooded murder? Sabrina is determined to discover the truth - even if it means enlisting the help of a spirit from beyond the grave.

PISCES:
A DREAMER, KNOWS SECRETS
SIXTH SENSE

*P*hoebe is a loner. She can sense when something's wrong, but people distrust her and are afraid of her premonitions. When Mark Chenier disappears, images grow in Phoebe's mind – she knows where Mark is, but no one, except her Cajun grandmother, believes her. Can she prove that she is right and that her 'dreams' really tell the truth?